Flags, Whistles, and Falling for the Ref

A Cornerstone Field League Story

Flags, Whistles,

and FALLING for the REF
A Cornerstone Field League Story

By: Jenny Beth Hall

For information address:
Jenny Beth Hall
C/O Mountains & Magnolias Publishing
932 Oldham Dr, Box 384, Nolensville, TN 37135
Published by:
Mountains & Magnolias Publishing
Amazon Ebook ASIN: B0GSMRXY3W
Amazon Paperback: 979-8-2509457-3-8
Ingram Spark ISBN: 979-8-9991894-8-6

First Edition April 2026

MORE BOOKS BY JENNY BETH HALL

Strike Team Faith Series
Smoke & Ember
>*Now available in Audiobook narrated by Samantha Silvia.

Finding Wren
>*Coming soon to Audiobook

Tex & Bea – 2026

Stand Alone Books
Christmas Storm at Kentucky Lake

Too Grumpy for Cupid
>*Now available in Audiobook narrated by Laurie Mullinax

DEDICATION

Hello Reader!

I am so glad you are here! This sweet little book has been so much fun to write and I look forward to hearing if you enjoyed it. It includes topics of faith, friendship, family, and of course, flag-football. But before you get to the story, here are a few fun facts:

☺ Flag-football is the fastest growing sport in the United States for girls.
☺ It is now an official NCAA emerging sport.
☺ The sport will debut at the 2028 Olympics.

I was so happy to be a part of our churches inaugural women's flag-football team several years ago. Since then, the league has grown by leaps and bounds. Even though I am not currently playing, I can't help but cheer them all on every time I see them out on the fields.

To my own Coach Emily and to Pastor Ryan who

has driven the success of the flag-football team and spread the word of God, thank you both for all you are doing… and for reading this book ahead of time.

Get out and play, but don't forget to pray.

Love,
JB

A NOTE ON LANGUAGE

You will notice a few Spanish words and phrases throughout this book. They are used intentionally to reflect culture, character, and connection.

Each word or phrase is simple and placed in context making it clear without translation. If you're unfamiliar with Spanish, don't worry, you won't miss the heart of the story.

CONTENTS

PROLOGUE

Sidelined

Sara

By the time I realized how bad things had gotten, it was too late. It all started crumbling long before it started falling apart. I told myself it was a pivot—an opportunity to learn something new. Now I just needed to convince myself of that.

My phone stopped ringing, business started slowing, and my email box flow was less than a trickle.

Meetings were cancelled. Deadlines were missed. Everything I had built suddenly became rubble.

Now there was just time. Too much time.

I wasn't sure what came next. I didn't have a plan. I sat staring at the laptop on the counter—it was the only solid surface left in this shoebox hotel room I found myself in the last few days.

On the floor, my suitcase sat open behind me. It was half packed, like I couldn't decide if I was staying or going.

My phone lit up beside me, buzzing on the counter, breaking through the silence.

Hannah. My best friend.

I let it ring on. Afraid of having to explain what I was walking through, and how I had ended up here. Alone. Broke. Scared. Unsure of myself.

The phone buzzed again. This time I picked it up.

"Hey," I said, trying to sound like myself.

"Hey, girl," Hannah's sweet voice trickled through the speaker warm and inviting, like she always was. "Haven't heard from you lately. You alive over there?"

"Barely," I said, surprised at the honesty I let squeak through my lips.

Hannah doesn't laugh. She's known me long enough to hear and know without me saying more.

"Okay," her voice was gentle. "Talk to me."

I leaned back against the counter, the artificial light buzzing, and not helping my mood. "I don't even know where to start."

"Pick a place. We can pick up the pieces from there as we need."

So, I did.

Not all of it. Some of it was too messy and

complicated. I didn't have words for some of it yet. But she heard enough to know what I wasn't saying.

"I thought I had it figured out," I admitted, the weight of it pressing in on me.

"For a season, you did. But seasons change."

"It doesn't feel like that. It feels like I missed something. Like I am missing something."

"Maybe. But perhaps you learned what you needed from that season and in the next, you will learn something else. Maybe it's time to move out of our hometown and spread your wings."

Hannah's words hit. Move. I hadn't even thought about that.

"I don't even know where to start with that. Like how does one just… move?"

The small pause on the other end of the phone told me she was thinking before she ever said anything.

"I have an idea," she said, with a hint of either genius or mischief—that would likely be determined later.

"Hear me out. This area is growing rapidly, there's lots of room for growth. And… we have a flag-football team at my church."

My curiosity was piqued, "You're inviting me to move with the kicker that there is a flag-football team?"

"Well, when you put it like that…yes. You don't have to have it all figured out. It doesn't even have to be long term. Just come to Tennessee and breathe for a while."

It sounds simple, but it meant admitting I wasn't rooted here anymore—and I didn't have a reason to stay. It meant stepping away from all that I knew: people, places, and relationships.

I looked around the hotel room again, dark, half packed suitcase, and full of the few possessions I had left—which wasn't much.

"I don't know if I will fit there," it hurt to say that. Hannah loved it there, but she had Jason, and her church.

"You don't have to fit, Sara. Just show up."

No expectations. No proving. No pretending like I had it together.

Just. Show. Up.

I took a deep breath and looked up like I could see to the heavens and ask God for advice, without actually asking. When I let the air I had been holding out, I took a chance.

"Okay," I said.

"Okay?" Hannah responds with a blend of excitement and disbelief.

"Yes, okay."

Hannah squeals on the other end of the line. "Oh, Sara! I am so excited!"

"I just have an important question," I am

already packing in my mind.

"Sure, what's up?"

"When does flag-football start?"

CHAPTER 1

First Impressions Matter

Sara

If you want to meet people quickly, apparently you let them rate you in something athletic in broad daylight. That's what I'm doing in Hannah's backyard.

Nearby her husband is at the grill—it's smoking like a small, controlled fire. The air smells like burgers, sunscreen, and summertime. Lawn chairs are lined up in the shade; some spouses and kids hanging out as the women prepare to practice. A speaker on the porch is playing something upbeat and wholesome—on brand for Hannah's world.

We had grown up in church and school back home in Texas. My family was from there, but we spent the first ten years of my life following my dad's job around before he came home and set up shop.

Hannah had been assigned as my school buddy for the first few days to help me get around. The two of us had several classes together and similar interests, which was anything we could compete at. We played every sport together we could and when we weren't competing, we were planning on it.

"This is Sara, my friend from Texas." Hannah introduces me to the group like she's presenting a prized recruit. "She was a major athlete back home and in college. Won all kinds of awards and got a scholarship; she's basically a machine." She hugs me from the side and beams with something that resembles pride.

I shoot her a look before I respond— slightly louder than necessary, "Do not set me up like that."

Hannah grins brighter. "I'm not setting you up. I'm hyping you. Consider me your number one hype girl." She winks before disappearing into the sea of women who are gathering to greet me.

The women from Hannah's team—Summer Breeze apparently—cheer, clap, and greet me like I'm a celebrity. Perhaps they don't realize the truth: I am a twenty-something woman who moved states because I needed a reset and couldn't stand to hear my own name in the same place where I'd been humiliated. I take a deep breath, smile, and take it all in.

"Texas!" one of them says, Rachel I think is her name, smiles wide. "We got ourselves a ringer."

"I am not a ringer," I insist, but it comes out weaker than I intend because they're all so... genuinely excited to have me here. That is more of a first for me than I want to admit to, so I don't.

Emily, the coach, steps forward with the energy of someone who has coached little league, managed a church bake sale, and organized an entire household before breakfast. She's all business without being mean about it and a natural-born leader. Her smile greets you before she does.

"You ever played flag-football?" she asks.

"I played where I used to live," I answer. "Not like… legit. But I know the basics." That's as much as I am willing to say for now, some things are better kept to yourself in the beginning.

"Good," Emily says, tossing me a set of flags like she's arming me. "Then we're going to see what you do when you've got someone coming for your hip."

"Is that a threat?" I ask suspiciously but a small, playful smile spreads across my face.

"It's more of an invitation," she replies walking toward the makeshift field, and all the listeners in earshot laugh.

I clip the belt around my waist and bounce lightly on the balls of my feet. I haven't worn these cleats in a while and almost didn't pack them when I moved, now I am glad I did. It felt good to put them back on and lace them up. Inside, that competitive fire just got stoked. I temper myself; a reminder that I don't have to show all my cards today, only enough to be invited back.

Hannah's backyard isn't long enough to 'go deep', but it's enough for a route or two. Hannah's dog wanders by, tail wagging, before getting shooed away from the makeshift end zone that's marked with two cones.

"This is a casual practice," Hannah says, leaning close as we walk onto the field. "Don't go full Texas."

"I don't know what that means," I say casually, but she's played other sports with me, so she knows that I know exactly what that means.

She points at my face with an accusatory smile. "That. That look means full Texas." I stifle a smile before it can break.

Emily claps her hands. "Alright. We're doing a few quick drills. Hannah, you snap. Rachel, you rush. Sara, you're running the route."

My stomach flips. Not fear—at least not exactly. It's more like… I forgot what it felt like to be new: watched, assessed, judged. There's no hiding behind polite conversation in sports. You either move like you know what you're doing, or you don't. I am acutely aware that everyone is watching.

Hannah crouches. "Ready?"

"Always." I can't help but let a smile cross my face now; the fire in me just blazed.

The snap is clean. I take the handoff and cut right, then left, and suddenly it's easy. My body remembers the moves like riding a bike. The grass practically glides under my cleats as I move last minute to avoid a defender—it's the split second when I decide—Rachel lunges for my flags and I spin away, laughing without meaning to as Rachel hits the ground.

"Oooh!" one of the spouses hollers from the sideline.

"Okay, Texas!" Hannah shouts, but I am still running to the end zone. Practice makes a better athlete.

I pass the cone, pivot, and sprint back, heart thumping in my chest in the best kind of way. Emily calls out corrections. Rachel grins and nods like she wants to take me down properly next time—just for fun. The women cheer like I've been part of this for months, not minutes.

When I slow to a stop, breathless and warm, Hannah and the others high five me. Even some of the spouses shout accolades.

"Told you," Hannah says. "You belong right here—even if it is just for now." She whispers that last part, knowing full well that my future is uncertain here.

We run more plays, and each time I let a little more of my skills out. By the end of the practice, we have all worked up an appetite and are ready to eat. I step back to watch this group gather: their laughter, the effortless way they all move around each other. Something in me loosen. They've welcomed me with open arms.

"Alright, Sara, tell me more about where you learned those skills you casually didn't tell us you had," Emily tosses me a red apple from the table and I catch it.

Nearby several other players are starting to gather in the line for food. They each lean in a little to hear our conversation.

"I am sure Hannah told you we played in school," I bite into the apple and it's crisp, juicy, and a perfect way to settle the hunger pains, and nerves, rising in my gut. The smell of the grill nearby has had me salivating.

"She said she played, but she didn't say 'And my awesome friend Sara is amazing!' or anything." Rachel says as she steps to Emily's left.

"I like to play, and I play hard. If I can contribute to the team, I would be happy to," I mean that, so I say it with a genuine smile.

"Well, I speak for all of us when I say we would love to have you play on our team. So, you want to be part of Summer Breeze?" Emily's question hits me in the gut as I look around at the women, each anxiously awaiting an answer from me.

Hannah is smiling at me from a few people back in line, nodding her head. Rachel crosses her arms over her chest with a look that teases, 'you know you want to.'

I finally answer, "I would love to play with y'all."

A resounding "Welcome to the team!" sounds from all of them.

Maybe this is what Hannah meant: '*It's not church, but community… people who show up.*'

"You're fast," Emily says, approving. "Running back for sure."

I blink. "Already assigning me a position?"

"Yes," she has that coach tone for sure. "Why wait?"

I try not to smile too much; just enough to acknowledge her comment.

I'm not here to get attached. I'm not here to rebuild my identity around a team. But my body—the traitor that it is—feels alive with this group.

And for the first time since I left Texas, my

laughter doesn't sound forced.
It sounds like me.

CHAPTER 2

Coin Toss

Sara

Work calls again, but when you're self-employed, it never stops. Calls, emails, coffee, marketing, development, and a human resources team of one. Sometimes I miss the old job, but more often than not, I don't.

The one thing I did glean from leaving Texas was writing my own rules and developing my own playbook. The downside though, is that starting over in unfamiliar territory meant re-explaining what I do to everyone I meet and convincing new people to buy in. Today's meeting had gone well, and I felt good they would sign on, but it had also been mentally exhausting. By the time I get to practice, I'm beat. Thankfully, this group of women always energizes me without even trying.

It's our first game: Summer Breeze vs Southern Lightnin'. Closing the tailgate and heading toward the fields, these teams couldn't look more different. Summer Breeze is bright colors—turquoise and bright orange—while Southern Lightnin' is black with white accents. All the jerseys bear the patch of the Cornerstone Field League, bearing a small cross and four stars on the top.

Summer Breeze looks like they're getting ready for a picnic, calm, cool, and collected. Each player doing some individual exercises. On the other side of the field though, Lightnin' is doing jumping jacks together, sounding off to a cadence.

"Oh boy," I say to no one but myself, or so I thought.

"Don't let them intimidate you. Their

coach was a drill sergeant in the Marine Corps and coaches like it." A tall man in a dark blue shirt is walking nearby on my right says.

"Not intimidated. Just taking note of the differences."

"Um-hmm. Famous last words," he smirks as he continues walking, his long strides pushing him ahead of me quickly.

He's tall and slender, but definitely athletic. As he walks away I take note of the bag on his shoulder—must be a spouse of one of the Lightnin' girls.

"Five minutes, coaches!" he hollers as he gets near the field. "Coach Emily, Coach Mel, y'all good?"

Emily, and the woman I assume is Mel, give a thumbs up and gather their teams in. I hustle over to join in.

"Alright y'all, we have a great plan. We have been practicing for weeks. We are ready!" Emily hypes the team, every woman has their game face on, and our hands pile in the middle of the circle.

Hannah calls out our chant, "Summer Breeze on 3! One, two, three—"

"Summer Breeze!" We all cheer and throw our hands up.

Around the field there are chairs, a small set of bleachers, and lots of spectators on their feet. Men, women, kids, old, young, and everything in between. Some of the men who play in the next game are already here around the field. I do like how this league supports each other.

The women's league has twelve teams, and the men's teams have over forty. There's a lot to be said about playing flag-football in a league, but when you realize this all started at a church and grew into this in a few short years—Hannah had told me the story one night—it is inspiring.

Both teams line up at center field, shoulder to shoulder, except the coaches. Coach Emily and Coach Mel meet the referee in the middle. It's the same guy from earlier, but now he's in stripes. Fantastic, the ref heard me sizing up the other team. He's the one person I don't want to know what I am thinking.

"Alright ladies, before we get started I am going to say a prayer," everyone bows their heads, I do the same. "Lord thank you for a beautiful evening to get in some football. Please watch over and protect each of these ladies as they play tonight and every night. We are grateful for the opportunity you have provided for them to do so. And Lord, help us refs to make good calls, and the ladies to know we are doing the best we can"—snickers escape from some lips, and I wonder what that was about—"Amen."

"Amen."

Everyone lines up after the coin toss; Lightnin' gets the ball first. On the snap, a tiny runner sneaks past me so fast I practically whirl in my shoes. Our defender—Miranda—hot on her tail. In three strides, Miranda's got her flag.

"Got you boo!" Miranda says with a laugh as she stops and embraces the tiny runner that squeaked by; I am going to have to watch that one.

"That's Rylie, but we call her Speedy," Hannah says next to me. "You will never see her coming until you feel the wind she leaves in her wake."

"You could have warned me," I huff a laugh.

"Nah. Then I would have missed the look on your face!" She hustles back to her spot on the far side of the line.

The next play, I have my eyes on Speedy, but they throw the ball to a woman near Hannah who grabs her flag and downs her before she gains yards. We high five and reset. We shut down their advance and take the ball back.

We huddle before the snap, and Emily calls the plays. "We are going to test their defenses the first two plays with exactly what they would expect, then we are going to let Texas loose," she glances to me before looking around the huddle; everyone nods before we break.

After two more plays we find their weak link, the brunette on the right side. I switch places with Claire last minute and when Emily snaps I go long, not even looking until I know I am clear. She overshoots by a hair: I jump for it—and keep running. Speedy is on my tail and I kick it up a notch.

The whistle blows and the ref hollers, "Touchdown."

The team bursts into excitement, and I can't hold back a big smile and throw my hands in the air. After some hugs and celebration, I toss the ball to the ref.

"Tone it down, or you'll be called for unsportsmanlike conduct," he says sternly, but with a smirk that I can't help but notice.

"Give her a break ref, she's new. We will

celebrate her!" Emily practically taunts him.

"You know the rules, Coach Emily," he shouts back.

"Oh, I do. I know you do too. But this one," she puts her arm around me, "she's on my team and we will celebrate her any way we want to!"

The ref shakes his head and walks away, volleying back and forth with Emily. It's a fun exchange between them, and some other players jump in accordingly. Apparently this is the rule following ref with no room for error. Great. Now I am on his radar.

By the fourth quarter we are up by seven. Lightnin' has the ball and Speedy is all over the field, changing positions every play.

"Sara," Emily calls me to her and pulls me in close. "Lightnin' will always throw to Speedy when they're facing a loss. Every single time. I need you to cover her, Hannah will back you."

"You got it Coach," I nod and take my place, quietly telling the player to my left to swap with me.

Speedy sees me move, and she does the same. We lock in when her team snaps the ball. I don't follow her directly, and the second she spent looking for me coming up on her tail cost her. As I close in from her other side—having gone the long way—I reach to grab her flag.

As I am about to grab her flag she spots me, and bolts. My miss on her flag sends me leaning too far forward and I manage to take her down in a full tackle instead; the whistle blows and the ref is on his way over. He blows the whistle again, like we didn't all hear it the first time.

"I am so sorry," I tell Speedy as I extend my hand to help her up.

"No worries. It happens." She heads over to where her coach is giving me the stink eye.

"Illegal contact—defense," the ref calls out.

"It was an accident!" I say loud enough for everyone to hear.

"You wrapped the runner instead of pulling the flag. Ten yards and an automatic first down," the Lightnin' teams sideline hollers in celebration.

"Now who's got unsportsmanlike conduct," I glare at the ref, but my look does nothing to penetrate those golden eyes.

Southern Lightnin' now has field advantage, and if we don't stop this advance, we lose. My tank feels empty suddenly, I know I let the team down.

"Thanks, ref," I say it with ire in my voice.

"Following the rules, nothing personal," his voice is firm.

Emily jumps in then, "Come on ref, you know it was an accident."

"Doesn't matter, Coach Emily. You know I run a tight ship."

"Sorry coach," I try to smile at Emily, but I feel depleted.

"Meh, no worries. It's all for fun, but we do like to win. Let's give it another shot." She pulls me back into the huddle like I didn't almost cost us the game.

Two more plays go by, and they have avoided throwing to Speedy. I can feel it coming though as I remember what Emily said about Lightnin' always defaulting to her in a pinch.

On the snap, I get in behind her and she's darting down the field not looking back; they're going for the long play. I glance back when she does and see the ball coming. She might be short and fast, but I am tall and have long arms. We both jump for it, but I reach up and my fingers tip the edge of the ball—right out of Speedy's reach.

The ref's whistle blows, and I smile at

Speedy, who suddenly looks very annoyed with me. That tip wraps it up for us, a win—even if it's just a scrimmage.

"Nice game," I tell her before heading back over to where Summer Breeze has gathered.

The women all cheer and applause as we celebrate before we join the good-game line; the one where both teams line up and slap hands and everyone repeats "good-game" until the last two people meet. As Speedy approaches she smiles a competitor's smile and points at me.

"I got my eye on you, Texas," she says as she high fives me instead.

"Same, Speedy."

Both women's teams gather after the game for a Bible study while the men's teams warm up. Several of the women have husbands playing in the next game and are excited to see what their teams have put together for the evening.

The Bible study this week is in the book of Hebrews, and Coach Mel reads it aloud.

"See to it, brothers and sisters, that none of you has a sinful, unbelieving heart that turns away from the living God. But encourage one another daily, as long as it is called 'Today,' so that none of you may be hardened by sin's deceitfulness. We have come to share in Christ, if indeed we hold our original conviction firmly to the very end. Hebrews 3:12-14."

Emily speaks up then, "We hope you all know that we pray for these teams, this community, and our church, every day. Each of you means so much to us. We hope that whether you are on the field or off the field, you find encouragement around you."

It feels good to be around women, and people in general, who are supportive and kind. They have welcomed me with open arms, even if Speedy does have her eyes on me. Internally I chuckle at that last part.

The men's game is about to start, and we move back to the sidelines. Some women have husbands on both teams that are scrimmaging, but some people are just here to do recon for their own teams. Who knew that church flag-football could be so competitive?

There's a new ref on the field, he's way shorter than the one that had been out there before, and definitely not as tan. I also notice that Speedy gives him a hug and a kiss on the cheek; alright that makes sense in my head. Wonder if he is fast too.

The men's game is fun to watch and just as competitive as the women's. Each team seems to have their own tricks and flairs. Like the ref from our game, he doesn't just run fast, he leaps over a guy on the field and lands on his feet to score a touchdown.

"If you call the short, fast girl Speedy, then what do you call him?" I ask Hannah as I point to the ref.

"Oh, that's just Ref," Hannah says.

"Unless he's on my nerves," Emily speaks up from two chairs down. "Then he's Captain Compliance or Rulebook Ralph."

"Or The Rule Ranger!" The short ref that just hugged Speedy says before he takes a drink from his water bottle during a time out.

"I heard that!" the ref says as he looks up from his teams huddle nearby.

The sideline bursts into laughter.

"But really, his name is Carlos," Hannah says.

CHAPTER 3

It's Only Paper

Sara

Today is a good day. I not only closed the biggest deal I have made since I moved to Tennessee, but it's the biggest deal I have ever closed. It feels good.

Working as my own sales rep has its difficulties, but I'm getting the hang of it. When the client asked for an agreement today, I was glad I had the forethought to prepare one in advance. The signed contract in my briefcase felt like gold. I needed to tell someone.

The phone rang twice before my dad answered. "Hey Dad!"

"Hey, sugar. How are things going?" Dad sounds like he's outside.

"It is going really well. I got a signed deal today, my first big one."

"That's fantastic! Hey Jeanie—" Dad hollers at my mom, "Sugar got a deal!"

In the background I hear her celebrate for me before he comes back on the line. "I am glad you are doing well. You sound good."

"I've made some good friends here. I am going back to church. I'm playing ball again," I tell him hoping he will ask, but he doesn't. "Flag-football."

"That's great Sugar. Listen Momma and I are walking into the opry house, so call us later."

"Sure Dad. Love you." I try to say it with a smile so he doesn't hear my disappointment, but I don't think he would notice disappointment if it hit him in the face.

Our call ended as quickly as it started, leaving me alone in my celebration. I don't know what to think about that. My parents have always cheered for me, but often it felt like it was from a distance. Maybe it's the embarrassment I brought to the family though. Maybe they don't want to associate with me. To be honest, I can't blame them if that's the case.

Things back home didn't end well, and leaving may have made it worse. But at least there was no one banging at my door, and the phone stopped ringing incessantly. The new phone number I got when I made it here probably helped with that last one.

I message Hannah and ask if she can get together later, but she's busy. Emily and Rylie as well. Speedy and I had turned out to have a lot in common and struck up a friendship—when we don't have jerseys on. It just happened to be one of those days where everyone but me had something going on.

I decide to celebrate alone anyway—because I can. Delivery, an enjoyable book, and maybe seeing if I could find some art to order online. My apartment had less personality than a potato.

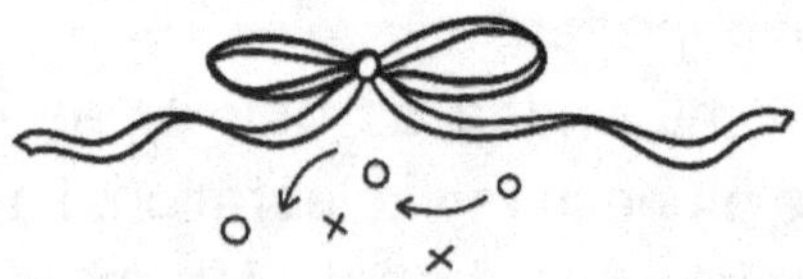

Delivery and sweet tea had been the perfect meal for me. I slipped into my comfy clothes and settled in with a book someone had suggested about a woman rediscovering who she was when she least expected to called *The Plans They Made Together*. I was in the latter half of the book and things were getting good. Her ex was almost out of the picture, and she was finding her voice; I could relate to that.

When the phone rang, I realized that I'd left it in the kitchen, and although the apartment was small, it wasn't that small. Getting up from my chair I moved to grab it quickly, but when I saw the caller's number, I silenced it and set it back down.

I don't know how he got this number, but I am not giving him a lick of my space today. I could deal with him later, or never if I tried really hard. As much as I wanted to keep reading, I knew I couldn't settle in with my feathers ruffled like they were. Instead, I reach for my anchor.

I had been thinking about something the Pastor had said a while back about vision. I grab my Bible from the desk—tags, notes, and pamphlets from church for the last decade or so poking out in all directions. In the small living room, I sit on the papasan chair, curled up and flip through the pages until I find it. Proverbs 29:18.

"Where there is no revelation, people cast off restraint; but blessed is the one who heeds wisdom's instructions." The notes written next to it read: Godly vision is always greater than our expectation (Eph.3:20). I flip to Ephesians next and read it out loud.

"Now to him who is able to do immeasurably more than all we ask or imagine, according to his power that is at work within us," I sit back and rest in those two verses.

I have a vision, but maybe I need to let God take control. Everything I had done to get what I wanted didn't seem to work in Texas. But now here, in Tennessee with this community that has been built around me, things seem to be going well. I bow my head to pray

"Lord, thank you for all that You are providing in my life. The people You have introduced me to. The business you continue to help me build. The way you hold me when I feel like I am standing alone. Please help me to hear your words and move forward with your vision in mind. Amen."

I had lost so much of my prayer life in the

last few years, and now getting it back felt good.

CHAPTER 4

Rules and Rebels

Carlos

If you want to be humbled, play flag-football with men who think they're still eighteen—and those who actually are eighteen.

I'm on the church field with the guys, sun dropping low enough in the west and turning the sky the color of cotton candy. We've got a decent turnout tonight, which means everyone's loud, competitive, and pretending they're just here for a good game while absolutely caring about a win.

"Ref!" Tyler calls across the line as I jog into position; even when I am a player, they still call me Ref. "You going to throw a flag on yourself for being late today?"

I don't look at him. "That's not how flags work, Ty. That's why I have to throw them on you every game."

The men in earshot laugh like they always do. They tease me about refereeing the women's games like I'm less of a player because I know the rules and actually enforce them. Some of the men here think a rulebook is a suggestion, but ask them about the Bible and they know the commandments. Football is simply different.

"Carlos knows the rules," Jason says dramatically. "Carlos *loves* the rules." I don't miss how he drags out the word *loves*.

"I love fairness," I correct him.

Tyler lifts his hands like he's preaching. "Listen to him. He's a man of order."

"You say it like it's a bad thing," I reply.

They line up. Ryan snaps the ball. I rush, cut inside, and snag the quarterback's flag clean.

"Down," I call, pointing at the spot.

Jason groans. "Of course you're calling it like you're in stripes." He shakes his head. "You should have a whistle for the men's games too."

"Who says I don't," I pull it out of my pocket and swing it around my fingers, a mischievous smile on my face. The men all howl.

"Bro," Tyler says through laughter. "Ref carries his whistle with him like a security blanket."

"I carry it because you all act like the rules don't exist on this field and someone has to keep you in line."

Tyler points at me while talking to Jason. "You see? This is why he refs the women. They actually listen."

"Barely," I mutter, thinking—against my will—about the new girl Hannah brought to the scrimmage last week. Sara, from Texas. Fast feet and sharp tongue. That woman argued a rule before she even learned everyone's names.

It should have annoyed me, and it did, but it also very much didn't. I like when people know the rules, and I like it even more when the women do.

Tyler catches my glance and smirks. "What's that look?"

"What look?"

"The one you get when you're thinking too hard."

I reset my stance and cross my arms over my chest. "Right now, I'm forcing myself to remember that this is flag-football and not tackle. That way when I chase you clowns down, I play by the rules."

Jason scoffs, "No, you're thinking about Summer Breeze," he's waggling his eyebrows.

I glare. "Do not start."

Jason's grin turns wicked. "Oh, we're starting. New girl on the women's team—Hannah's friend—we saw you glance twice."

I toss the ball back to the center harder than necessary. "She's competitive."

"She argued with you. How did that feel, Ref?" Tyler asks, delighted to be bulldozing me.

"She questioned the call," I correct.

"That's feisty," Tyler says.

I ignore them and motion for the snap. But I can't ignore the truth: I've been reffing long enough to recognize when someone plays like they're trying to outrun something bigger than the game. Sara plays like that and I wonder what she's running from. But I also can't forget the way she looked at me with those pretty blue eyes: daring, confident, and beautiful.

Tyler whistles through his teeth. "Carlos is interested."

"I am not," I respond too fast. They won't believe me either way.

Because when I glance toward the other side of the field—where the women practice on alternate nights—I find myself wondering if we'll see each other somewhere off the field. I wonder if she'll learn the league's culture, if she'll soften at all, and then I wonder why I care.

I don't need a distraction, and I definitely don't need complicated. And I don't need a woman who treats every scrimmage and drill like a championship game. Sara does all of the above. But as the guys keep chirping and the sun drops lower, I realize something simple.

I'm already paying too much attention to that blonde from Texas.

Tyler's toddler—wearing only a diaper and a t-shirt—bursts onto the field chasing a ball that rolled away from him.

"Hey, that's a live ball!" Jason shouts, laughing.

Tyler scoops him up with one arm and

proudly shouts, "Future quarterback!"

"He throws better than you already!" I holler at Tyler, mimicking a bad throw.

Everyone laughs, including Tyler.

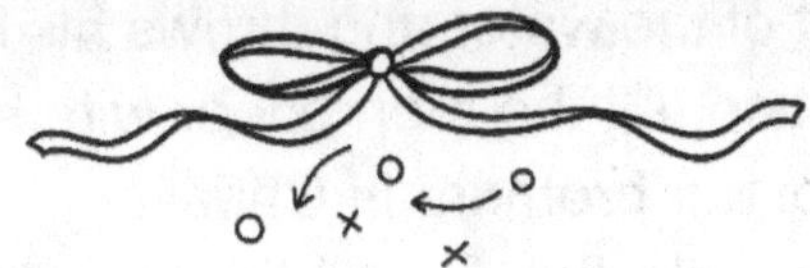

After practice we gather around for Bible study, and tonight's special event—Pastor Ryan is baptizing two men. This flag-football league has consistently grown in the number of teams, but it has also grown the number of souls in God's kingdom.

Ryan shares a word with the men's group "Galatians 6:2: Carry each other's burdens, and in this way you will fulfill the law of Christ. That is what we do on this field before and after games. Cornerstone Field League is more than football, it's a family. If you need something, we are here. Bring your good days, your bad days, and everything in between."

The message is a good word and reminds me of times when I wasn't in the place I am now. Looking back, I can clearly see the mountains and valleys. Right now, though, I am glad to be on a mountain top. But I know when I am in the next valley, this group will be there, and I will be there for them as well.

Ryan baptizes a guy named Mitch who comes out of the water and throws his hands up in celebration. All the men cheer with him; he is now one of our brothers in Christ.

This little flag-football league has taken on a culture of its own, especially when it's tied to faith and family. This field is often as much of a family reunion as it is a battlefield for souls.

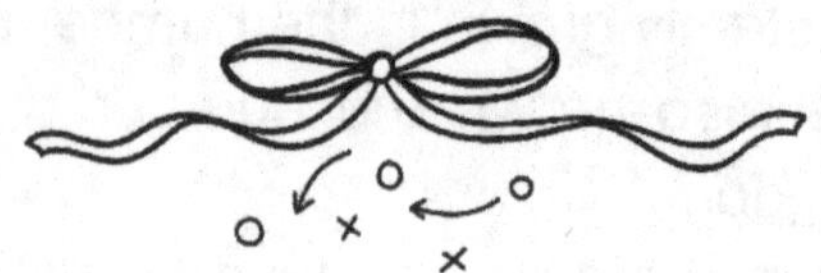

The gym bag makes a clunk on the floor as I drop it after closing the door. I flip the lights on before heading to the kitchen to refill my water bottle and grab a snack. Evening practices always leave me extra hungry.

A peanut butter and jelly sandwich and a small glass of milk are the perfect way to recover from a good workout. I don't even sit at the table, I just lean against the counter to eat before heading to the other room to catch the news while I read for a while. A few minutes in, a news story catches my ear.

"This week kicks off the start to the fastest growing girls sport in the country, and you will probably be surprised to find out what it is... when we come back."

I huff a small laugh already knowing what it is.

My siblings and I grew up playing soccer, but when my youngest sister found flag-football, she was immediately hooked. She was fierce and fiery but also cheered everyone else on. Shortly after that I realized it wasn't only her, all her friends were hooked too. The sport was growing big time for girls.

I look over at the picture of Marisol and I at the regional flag-football competition. She was in the pink uniform she loved, and I was in my first set of stripes. It was a privilege to be there and watch them win. She and her team were the reason I got into reffing; the girls wanted to play, but they couldn't find a ref. Our town was barely big enough for a full team, much less a ref, so I volunteered.

It was easy enough to learn since I already played with friends. It turned out it was great cross training for soccer. After a few classes at the recreation center, memorizing the rule book, and a new pair of cleats, our town now had a ref for their team.

After that, I was hooked on the game, and the stripes.

CHAPTER 5

Down on the Field

Sara

My apartment feels more like a hotel room than a home. It's clean, minimal, and mostly furnished with things that were easy to bring when I came. They're the same things that are easy to replace or leave behind if I had to. A small couch. A coffee table. A bistro-size kitchen table with two chairs I bought online because it seemed ridiculous to eat standing up forever.

But the walls are blank and industrial. There are no photos, no history, no story to tell. That's intentional. Because history has a way of catching up. I looked for art, but nothing has spoken to me.

I lace my shoes at the edge of the couch and check my calendar, as if I stared hard enough, I can control the next few months. Work has been full speed since I moved here, and that part I can handle. The job has always been predictable; effort equals results. It's the people who are the wild card.

I've been here long enough now that I've settled into an easy rhythm. I make my own schedule for work, so planning around any opportunities to hang out with Hannah or the other ladies is easy enough. Flag-football practices twice a week during the season; men and women on opposite nights. The coaches hold devotionals after games, and I've learned the art of slipping out before anyone asks me which service I attend or whose small group I'm in.

It isn't that I hate church, but that church can feel like a spotlight. People want to know you and bring you in, and right now I want to keep people at arm's length and not talk about the past. I've had enough spotlight in my life.

My phone buzzes.

Hannah: *Game tonight? Emily says she's putting you in at RB.*

I roll my eyes even though no one can see me.

Me: *I plan to be there.*

Hannah: *Cool. Also, we're grilling after. Come hungry.*

Grilling after. It's part of the package, and I am not sure if it belongs to the church, the team, or the league culture.

That's part of what I didn't expect about coming here: normalcy. The way these women argue over whose casserole is best, laugh at the way they play—while also breathing down each other's necks on the field—and the way they include me without demanding I explain myself. It's just 'come as you are.'

This should be easy enough to accept. For someone like me though? It's not.

Because back in Texas, I accepted inclusion once and it came with conditions. I accepted love and it came with expectations. And when I failed to meet the version of myself someone else wanted, I got replaced.

My foot taps against the floor—restlessness settling in. I stand and pace, then stop by the window. The parking lot is quiet, and anxiety is starting to creep in about belonging.

I tell myself I'm doing this league for social reasons. For networking and balance. That may be partly true, but if I'm honest…. I'm doing it because playing is the only place I still feel like myself without trying.

Football doesn't ask questions. It doesn't matter where you came from. And it doesn't look at you and decide you're too much. On the field, "too much" is useful; my intensity is an asset.

I grab my bag—light, efficient, everything in it arranged like I'm going into battle. Water. Tape. Extra socks. A sleeve brace I don't need but keep it anyway because I like feeling prepared.

As I lock my apartment door, a thought slides in uninvited.

What if this place becomes home?

The idea should feel comforting. Instead it feels like risk. Before I can think anymore, I shove the thought down and head for my car. Tonight is just another game. I have played under more pressure than this with fewer skills.

Just grass, other players, and the kind of

laughter that keeps trying to pull me into the circle; I can handle that. I can handle anything— or at least that's what I tell myself.

And maybe that's the problem.

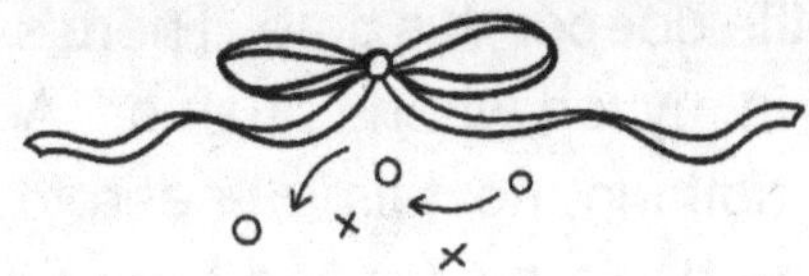

I knew something wasn't right immediately. It wasn't dramatic. There was no twisting collision or pileup. Just a sharp tug low in my calf when I cut right to dodge Hannah's block. It felt tight, like a rubber band stretched beyond its limits. I stumbled, caught myself, and jogged it off before anyone could make a big deal about it.

I've played through worse.

In Texas, I finished a soccer semifinal with a sprained ankle that looked like I shoved a grapefruit in my sock by halftime. I hit a triple in softball once with a bruised rib. I finished a half marathon with my hip partly dislocated. Pain doesn't stop me, so I walk it off.

Emily yells at me, "You okay Sara?"

I talk myself through the pain, but take a

moment to look her way and nod. She has that look all coaches have when they're not sure a player is being honest; questioning if I am okay and if she should step in.

The second play I feel it again, but the pain is a little deeper this time. There's a foreign weakness in my leg when I push off. Again, I tell myself it's nothing; next time I need to warm up more. We're down by six and I am not coming out of this game because my leg feels "off."

"Sara!" Emily calls from the sideline and shows me the sign for the next play.

I nod and get back in position. *My* position. They've assigned me running back; I have a team, and I might just belong here.

The snap is clean. I take the handoff and step through the gap that opened like it was designed for me. I plant my left foot to cut inside; my cleat sticks. For half a second, my body keeps moving but my foot doesn't. And then I hear it—POP!

My leg feels like someone kicked me hard in the back of the ankle. I turn, expecting to see a defender behind me, to my surprise, there's no one there.

My leg gives out and I hit the turf hard, the ball tumbling out of my arm. This time when

I try to stand, my leg doesn't respond like it should. It's like my foot and my brain are no longer connected.

I lie there, stunned, staring at the grass.

"Stay down!" Emily shouts sharply as she runs toward me, Hannah behind her.

"I'm fine," I tell them automatically, breathing through the pain.

"You are not fine," Hannah says crouching next to me.

I try to stand to prove them wrong. The second I put weight on it, I almost black out from the pain.

Emily's face shifts from coach-frustrated to genuinely concerned. "You're done," she says firmly. "Game's over for you, Sara."

"I can finish," I argue through gritted teeth.

"No," she's kneeling in front of me, a sad, concerned kindness on her face. "You're done." I hate those words more than the pain.

And that's when I see him, the referee— Carlos—is already walking toward us, whistle bouncing against his chest, expression unreadable but focused. He doesn't rush. He never rushes, and that is infuriating.

"What happened?" he asks, voice steady.

"She's done," Emily answers before I can.

"I'm not done," I snap, and it comes out harsher than I mean it to. "I'm sorry Emily." She nods and smiles.

Carlos kneels beside me. Up close, his eyes are more golden honey than I remember from our stare down during the scrimmage. He takes a look at my leg; assessing what he can see.

"Did you feel it before this play?" he asks.

I hesitate, and it's half a second too long, and when he ticks his head to the left expectantly, he knows.

"Yes," I admit. "It felt tight."

"And you kept playing." It isn't a question, but I feel judged.

I glare at him and speak through gritted teeth, "We were down."

His jaw tightens. "Tranquila. Did you hear anything?"

I swallow, holding back the pain and fighting back tears. "It popped."

He turns to look at me and the concern in his eyes sharpens, "May I touch your leg?"

I struggle to maintain my composure, but I nod. *God, please don't take the one thing I am still good at.*

Carlos lifts my leg behind the knee and gently runs his hand over my calf, looking with his eyes more than his hands. He sets my leg down gently and says quietly, "Don't move it."

"I can walk," an attempt to move is met by my body's refusal.

"You can't." It's a strong statement and he has no idea who I am and what I am capable of, but the confidence in his voice makes my stomach drop.

"I don't want help," I mutter.

He looks at me for a long second, and the way he studies me makes me feel seen in a way I don't particularly enjoy. Like he sees right through me.

"I know." His voice is soft. "But you might need it anyway."

CHAPTER 6

When it Snapped

Carlos

I saw it before she let on that there was a problem. She had stumbled two plays earlier and although she masked it well, I've played long enough to recognize compensation when I see it. Her stride shortened. Her push-off lost power. She shook her leg out between downs like she could intimidate it into cooperating.

She's stubborn. Competitive. Maybe even *too* competitive.

When she planted and went down without contact, I knew. Then the way she tried to stand and failed; I had no doubt.

I walk toward her with calculated steps because if I rush, everyone else will panic. It's part of the ref job—control the tone and you control the moment.

Coach Emily is already there at her side. Telling Sara she's out, I hear it from here. She's doing the right thing, even if Sara doesn't like it. And Sara is arguing, because of course she is. I hold in a laugh. This isn't funny, I know this is not a laughing matter—even if she is trying to prove she's strong.

"Did it feel like someone kicked you?" I ask Sara.

Her eyes widen slightly. "Yes."

Classic Achilles presentation, but I don't make that call. No matter my experience, it's not my role.

"I played soccer and football," I tell her evenly. "I've seen this before."

She studies me, searching for exaggeration. I don't give her any.

"Achilles?" she whispers the question like

she already knows how bad this could be.

"Possibly." I keep my tone and hold her gaze.

Reading her face, she is scared as the realization settles in. Her face changes. She sits there, still. All the fight has left her body.

Hannah squeezes her shoulder before standing, "I'll get ice."

"I can drive myself," Sara says confidently.

"You can't even walk," I reply calmly.

"I'll manage." Those blue eyes lock into mine and she tried to maintain control.

I see it in her face that she would try it, too. She would hobble herself there just to prove she could.

"You need to go to the hospital," Coach Emily says. "But I can't drive you; I rode with someone else."

"I'll take you to the emergency room," I say.

"You're the ref," Sara shoots back with disdain, "not my dad."

"No, I am not your dad," I agree. "But I'm responsible for this field, and you got hurt on it. Besides, there's other refs here and they can step in."

She looks at me like she wants to argue more, but something in her expression shifts. Beneath the fire, there's something much deeper: fear.

"I just moved here," she whispers, like she doesn't mean to say it out loud.

I nod once, "I know."

Hannah mentioned her friend would be moving here before Sara ever arrived. Said she was transplanting from Texas and would need to make some friends. Hannah knew if Sara came here she could have community, even if she wouldn't call it that.

"I don't need saving," the cracks of her façade start breaking as the pain wears her down.

"I'm not trying to save you," I tell her. "I'm trying to make sure you don't make it worse."

When I stand and offer my hand, she stares at it for a moment like I have issued a challenge instead of offering help. She exhales—long and shaky—before taking it. Even with the pain, her grip is strong.

"Listen, you shouldn't walk on it, even if you can. Let me carry you," I offer first. I don't want to caveman-style carry her, but part of me wants to. I already see how stubborn she is, and

I brace for her to argue.

"Okay."

"Okay?" I ask to make sure I heard her right.

"Yes," she looks up at me then, her blue eyes are bright as the sky, but full of emotion. Tears threatening to fall down her sun kissed cheeks. "But only after I get off this field and out of their sight."

There's something about her meeting me halfway that I realize is both strength and a weakness. Instead of arguing with her I put my arm around her to help her—but only until we are out of sight.

Everyone claps and hollers for Sara. Emily calls the team over for a huddle and prayer, Hannah promises to call her later, and I walk with Sara to my truck.

As I help her off the field and into my truck I remember something: cleats and stripes don't always play well together.

CHAPTER 7

More Serious than I Thought

Sara

    I refused the ambulance and let the ref take me—against my better judgment, but I wasn't going to be made a spectacle of. I wasn't going to let sirens pull into the church parking lot in the middle of a game while half the congregation watched from folding chairs. The thought of the prayer circle forming around me made me panic. After all, I had a friend that once hobbled two miles on a trail with a broken ankle, I could surely get myself where I needed to go.

"I'm fine," I say for the tenth time as Carlos helps me into the passenger seat of his truck. "It's just a sprain."

Carlos looks at me with a soft smile before shutting the door without responding. He's holding back, but I don't think I even believe this is a sprain anymore.

I'd heard someone begin praying while I was still sitting on the turf, trying my best not to cry. I don't do prayer circles. I don't do public vulnerability. I definitely don't do both at the same time. As we pull out of the parking lot I see they've all got their heads bowed in prayer as they start their devotion.

The ride to the emergency room is downright painful—and excruciatingly quiet. The hum of the old truck engine and the faint echo of worship music from the ancient speakers are the only thing keeping the truck cab from feeling like an empty chasm.

Carlos keeps glancing at my leg like he's calculating something. He's too calm, and it irritates me.

"You don't have to hover," I mutter.

"I'm not hovering."

"You're right. You're observing adjacently."

That earns the smallest hint of a smile and a nod.

When we pull into the emergency room, I reach for the door handle and let myself out. The moment my foot touches the pavement, pain shoots straight up my leg and I suck in a sharp breath that embarrasses me. Before I can protest, Carlos is around the truck, supporting me. His strong arms, holding my weight.

"Don't," he says quietly. "Let me help you."

"I can manage," I look up at him then, trying to look strong and independent.

He studies me for a long second, like he's weighing whether arguing is worth it. Then, without another word, Carlos bends down and lifts me. I don't even have time to protest.

My arms instinctively loop around his shoulders, but his hold on me is solid and secure. He doesn't even change his breathing, like this isn't even difficult for him. My pride flares, but it's drowned out by the steady rhythm of his heartbeat beneath my ear. He smells like the outdoors, spices, and something like adventure.

"You could have warned me," I mutter.

"You would've argued, like you argue about everything." He doesn't say it in a mean way. In fact, I think he is trying to be lighthearted right now.

I huff, but don't let go. He's helping me, and as much as I hate it, the pain is radiating and I don't have the energy. And he's right, I would have argued.

The automatic doors slide open, and I am acutely aware that I am being carried into the emergency room by the referee from the church's flag-football league while still wearing my jersey and cleats. This is not how I planned to meet people in this town.

He sets me down gently in a wheelchair without asking first.

"You're bossy," I tell him.

"You're injured," he replies. And this time, he smiles at me.

I really look at him then—at Carlos, and there's something in his expression I didn't notice before. He's not doing this from obligation. There's conviction in his eyes.

CHAPTER 8

Lean on Me

Carlos

She weighs less than I expected. Not physically—she's athletically strong—but in the way she goes still when I lift her. For someone who fights everything, she doesn't fight that.

I've carried patients before: fractures, heat exhaustion, panic attacks. There's a particular way the body settles when it knows it has to trust you. Professionally, I have seen it many times before—too many times to not recognize it when I see it.

The way she described the pop. The way her calf slackened when I supported her leg. The lack of a bulge in her lower leg. The fear she tried to mask.

If I'm right, and this is her Achilles, she's looking at surgery and months of recovery. For someone like her—fierce athletic, active, and on the go—this will feel like a prison sentence. I say a silent prayer as I push her toward the check-in desk. It's the kind of prayer that slips into my mind like an automatic thought.

Lord, thank you for putting me there on the field today. Thank you for her teammates and Coach Emily. Help the doctors and nurses to help her quickly. And if there is any way for me to be wrong, please make It happen. Amen.

She's scanning the waiting room like she's preparing for a battle. Fidgety, anxious, and wringing her hands.

"I could've walked," she tries to convince me.

"You would've fallen."

"I doubt that." She looks away as she says it, like she even doubts herself.

I glance down at her. "Need I remind you that you nearly passed out in the parking lot?"

She narrows her eyes. "That was strategic breathing."

I almost laugh. Even now, she refuses to surrender control.

After we get her checked in, I kneel in front of her so we're eye level. I keep my voice low and calm.

"I am going to ask you an important question: did you feel it give before the pop?" I ask.

Her jaw tightens and her answer is quiet as a mouse, "Yes."

"And you kept playing." I am not angry. I am not even upset, because I would have done the same thing once upon a time. But I am sad for her, that she felt she needed to—like she had something to prove.

Her eyes flash, but when she speaks her voice doesn't have the bite it did before, "We were down."

There it is again: that need to win, to prove. As if her worth on the field is more important than anything else.

"I've seen these types of injuries before," I say carefully.

She studies me before she responds. "From what? Watching internet tutorials?"

I hesitate and center myself. I don't usually lead with my job. It changes how people respond to you, and the questions they will ask you. But for her, I hope it calms her now.

"I work as a paramedic," I say finally. "When I'm not reffing."

Her expression shifts, a little shock and regret in it.

"I'm not guessing, Sara," I continue gently. "I want you to be able to mentally prepare."

"For what?"

"For the possibility that this is more than a strain." My words create a silence that stretches between us.

We stare at each other a few moments. Around us a nurse calls a name, a toddler cries, and the world keeps moving. This is just a moment, but it weighs heavy over her. I don't miss that.

Sara's shoulders slowly lose some of their tension. "I don't... have anyone here," she says quietly, not looking at me.

The honesty in that statement looks like it hits her harder than the injury.

"You do," I say before I overthink.

She looks up sharply.

"The Cornerstone Field League isn't just games," I continue. "It's community at the church. That's kind of the point."

She gives me a skeptical look. "I'm not exactly the church type. Don't get me wrong, I am a believer, but I don't need a church."

"That's okay." She searches my face for judgment and doesn't find any. "We're still going to show up. It's what we do."

For a moment, something soft flickers across her expression. It may not be belief or agreement, but it's an opportunity for all of us to be able to act on the words we say; to be the hands and feet of Jesus and show up when needed.

The nurse calls her name, and I rest a hand lightly on the back of her wheelchair.

"Ready?" I ask.

She exhales slowly, "No."

"Good," I say gently. "That means you understand what's at stake."

She rolls her eyes, but she doesn't push my hand away.

And as I wheel her toward the exam room, I realize something I didn't expect. I don't feel professionally responsible anymore, This feels personal.

I push her wheelchair down the hallway, trying to offer support until Coach Emily arrives—because I know she will. The hospital feels industrial: overbearing fluorescent lights overhead, the antiseptic smell that turns my stomach, and an eerie quiet amongst the beeps of machines. I try to keep the mood light.

"Y'all really like to keep this place inviting, don't you?" The nurse turns to me and gives me a sly smile before she motions for me to step away.

"I've got it from here," the nurse says, but I don't miss Sara looking up at me with concern.

I kneel down next to her, "I'll be right outside, cariño."

She nods once, pressing her lips together like she is afraid to speak.

"There's a chair in the small waiting area across the hall," the nurse says passively as she pulls the curtain closed behind them.

The waiting area is more of a hollowed-out room where chairs were pushed against the walls and a stack of magazines left on a tiny corner table.

I text Coach Emily: *They took her back. I*

think this is worse than it looks. Hopefully, she can update you soon.

Emily texts back quickly: *Thank you for taking her. I will get there soon.*

I don't usually pray out loud in hallways, but I also don't usually feel this responsible for someone I've barely known. Other than the few times she's been in my face about calls I made she didn't agree with, we have hardly talked. I feel called to take a minute to pray for her.

"Lord, I know You care about the big things and the small ones. This feels big to her. If this is going to be a long road, don't let her walk it alone. Give her peace and clarity. And if You're using this for something bigger, let it be. Amen."

I've learned working as a paramedic that bodies don't always respond to big prayers the way people want them to. What they do respond to is support, community, time, and patience. Sara's new here and she's going to need all of that and more.

The nurses and doctors come in and out of her room. I can barely hear them talking and try not to listen and break her privacy. There are certain words that I can't help but miss along the way though: suspected Achilles rupture.

The doctor offers her something for the pain but it's what he says to me when he comes out that surprises me.

"You must be the ref; she's asking for you." He doesn't stick around before he heads down the hall.

I stand, take a deep breath, and straighten my jersey before I head in. She's staring up at the ceiling looking defeated, but when she sees me come in, she wipes her tears away.

"How ya feeling?" I ask her as I take a seat in the chair next to her.

"Worthless," she looks everywhere in the room but at me.

"You are not worthless. You are inspiring on the field," I smile at her, but she rolls her eyes and looks away.

The nurse comes in a few minutes later and gives her some medicine. She begrudgingly takes it and the nurse mumbles, "Athletes," before she walks back out.

After a while I see her body relax, and I can tell her mind is also calming. Before I know it, her head collapses on her shoulder and she's sleeping. It doesn't look comfortable, so I open a cabinet in the room and find a sheet, refolding it to the size of a pillow and gently prop her head up.

She relaxes immediately, trusting the support. I gently push a loose hair behind her ear before I sit down.

"You're going to be alright," I murmur, mostly to the room.

I am sure she doesn't hear me, but I mean it.

A bit later, her eyes flutter open, but only long enough for me to see they look glassy; the medicine has definitely kicked in.

"Hi," the word is barely over her lips before she smiles at me—or at least tries to smile. I won't tell her, but she looks like she might have drool in the corner of her mouth.

"Hey," I say softly, not sure if she is awake or not.

She blinks up at me, like she's trying to clear the fog. "Did you… pray?" Her voice is full of curiosity mixed with heaviness of sleep.

"Yes." I answer honestly. I have nothing to hide.

"For healing?"

"Not quite. For peace and for community."

"That's different."

"Healing is the doctor's job. Peace is God's," I tell her quietly.

She studies me like that answer matters before she nods off. This time though, her head falls gently on the makeshift pillow.

Sometime later she starts talking, barely able to keep her eyes open. Her words are not understandable at first, but they clear up. I am not sure she even knows she is talking—much less to me—but I listen. She looks at me with a lopsided smile before she starts talking.

"Texas was loud," she murmurs.

"What do you mean?"

"Everything was loud. Expectations. People. My family." Her words drift in and out like she's trying to hold onto them. "They loved the athlete version of me. The strong one. The winning one."

I don't interrupt her, just let her speak. Her eyes close again as she looks like she has drifted back to sleep, until she mumbles again.

"I was engaged," she whispers.

Those words land heavier than her diagnosis.

"He loved the athlete too," she continues, voice thick with medication and memory. "But not the rest of me." She pulls the flat sheet on the bed up, balling it in her fist like a security blanket.

My chest tightens; this is personal.

"He cheated," she adds, almost clinically. "With someone softer. Someone less competitive. Said I was exhausting." A small, broken laugh slips out. "He wasn't wrong."

I move closer to her and take her hand. "He was wrong," I say quietly.

Her eyes flutter again and drift toward me but don't quite focus.

"I left before the wedding," she murmurs. "Packed up my apartment. Took a job transfer. Came here because Hannah said her church was great and flag-football was fun. Low pressure with a side of community." Her mouth twitches, fighting back emotion. "I didn't plan on rupturing anything."

The vulnerability in her voice is raw, unguarded. She would never say this unmedicated and fully awake.

"You're not exhausting," I tell her softly. "You're intense. There's a difference."

She gives the faintest hum of disagreement. "Don't tell them," she whispers.

"Tell who?"

"The church girls. I have been someone's

'cause' before."

I almost smile.

"You won't be a cause," I make the quiet promise, but I am not sure she hears me.

Her breathing evens out slowly after that and she's asleep again. I feel the weight of what she entrusted to the air between us; she may not have even realized I was in the room. That's when Coach Emily and Hannah show up.

I hold my finger to my lips, and they stop at the door. Hannah peeks in to check on her friend, but doesn't come in. With Sara sleeping, the three of us step into the hallway.

Hannah says she called Sara's parents and they basically wrote it off as a "bad day." That frustrated me and I immediately commit to showing up, because I have seen too many patients struggle alone. Not on my watch. Besides, my shifts are sporadic enough that I have some time to give, and I know these ladies will give all they can.

We agree that it's best if Hannah is there when she wakes up. She may not have meant to tell me the things she did, and I don't want her to be embarrassed if she realizes it. Her confession is safe with me.

She came here to outrun something.

Now she can't run at all. And I have the steady belief that this injury isn't random. It's not punishment, just cosmic irony.

CHAPTER 9

Package Deal

Sara

My leg feels like it's both dead and burning simultaneously. Crawling out of the abyss of sleep, I remember yesterday and cringe; I don't know how I am going to do this alone.

"Good morning, sunshine!" Hannah's voice is bright and full of cheer, and while I normally love that, today I want to tell her to get lost, but I don't.

"Morning." I sit on the edge of the bed, feeling the full weight of my leg hanging down. I try to move my foot, hoping that yesterday was a bad dream, but the deadweight tells me I am wrong. I let out a groan and rub my hands over my face.

"Wanna talk about it?" she asks, sitting on the edge of my bed.

"It all feels like a blur. I felt like I was making headway here. I closed a big deal, I made some friends, and I was having fun. Now I don't know what I will do."

"Pray first, and trust God to guide your path." She takes my hand and leads us in a short prayer. Her words remind me of a voice in the distance: Carlos. "—Amen."

"I think Carlos prayed for me yesterday," I tell her, not sure what to think about it or about telling her.

Hannah stands from the bed and turns to me with a smile. "That wouldn't surprise me. As much as we give him grief for being a rule follower, he's also a good man. God first always. Everything else after that. Rules forever."

That last one makes me huff a laugh,

"What did y'all call him? The Rule Ranger?"

"Among other fun names." She gives me her hand to help me stand. "But he is a really nice guy. If he prayed, it was from his heart."

I roll my eyes, but I can't verbally deny that. Yesterday he was so kind and sweet, even if his rules get on my nerves.

"By the way," Hannah's demeanor changes, "he's going to meet us at your appointment. I got a call from work and can't get out of it, but I can get you there."

Hannah looks bummed, and I am sure she is. I debate calling a cab, but Carlos has given me no reason to disrespect his time.

"Thank you, Hannah. I know you have a life."

"Girl, you are part of it. I am so glad you're here, but I hate that this is your plight," she pulls me in and squeezes me.

"I called your parents, by the way." Her tone changes and I don't have to guess what that means.

"How did that go?"

"If I said, same parents, different day, what would you think?" Her eyes are sad, but honest.

I shrug, "Unfortunately, I am not

surprised. I know they're enjoying their lives, but I wish they could be present. Ya know?"

"I know. But you have me!" she grins with a cheesy smile as she helps me up and we finish hobbling together to the kitchen.

Hannah's right. Our friendship spans almost our entire lives. Without her friendship, I don't know where I would be.

Carlos sits next to me in the waiting room. I almost didn't recognize him when we got here. Nice jeans, a polo shirt with a Spain logo, and a backwards baseball hat—his dark hair sticking out the front. I can't help but notice that it's so dark that when the light hits it, the black looks navy. Like the reflection of an oil slick.

"No ref stripes today?" I ask him, trying to make light of the situation.

"Only on the field. Believe it or not when I am off the field, I am just Carlos. Paramedic by day, Referee by night," he puts his hands on his hips and smiles like a superhero. There's a genuineness to it.

When the nurse calls me back, I ask Carlos to come too. He said he had seen these injuries before, so his opinion will be appreciated. Besides, it's good to have someone with medical knowledge in my corner to explain anything I might not understand.

The orthopedic surgeon doesn't waste any time at my appointment. He pulls up the imaging and shows me the gap like it's a broken zipper inside my own body.

"It's a full rupture," the surgeon says calmly. "Complete tear of the Achilles tendon. The good news is you're young, healthy, and active. Surgical repair has excellent outcomes."

Excellent outcomes. It echoes through my head.

"That means what exactly?" I ask.

"It means with surgery and proper rehab, you can return to sports and activity. But we're looking at a long road."

"How long?"

"Six to nine months before competitive return. Twelve months, maybe longer, before it feels fully normal."

Twelve months. It takes everything in me not to flinch.

"Non-weight-bearing for at least two weeks," he continues. "You'll be in a splint initially, then a boot with heel wedges. Physical therapy begins early, but progression is gradual. If you push too fast, you risk re-rupture."

He looks at Carlos. "Does she have good support at home?"

I open my mouth to answer, but the surgeon keeps talking—to Carlos. The only reason he's even here is because everyone else has been busy and he happened to be free. Otherwise, Hannah would be here, or Emily, or anyone but the guy who smells like sports, summer, and the outdoors all at once.

"You'll need to help her with stairs, bathing, meals for the first week especially. She won't be able to drive for several weeks." The sound of the doctor talking to Carlos pulls me back to the conversation.

Carlos nods once, not missing a beat. "Understood."

The surgeon smiles at him. "Good. It makes a significant difference when the boyfriend is involved."

My jaw drops, Carlos blinks, and we both start speaking at the same time, "We're not—"

The surgeon chuckles. "Happens all the

time. Fiancé then?"

"No," I say quickly, heat crawling up my neck. "He's the referee."

There's a pause as the doctors eyes flit from Carlos to me and back again.

"…Of the church's flag-football league," Carlos clarifies.

The surgeon looks mildly surprised, then amused. "Well. Good referees make good calls—and they follow the rules."

I refuse to look at Carlos, the heat in my cheeks is enough to make me want to find a closet to hide in until it goes away. Dying of embarrassment was not on my bingo card today, or this year. So far, I am zero for two.

The rest of the consultation blurs. Surgery is scheduled for first thing Friday morning. They'll do an open repair, stitching the tendon ends back together. I'll go home same day if there are no complications.

Same day surgery: like this is routine. Like my entire identity isn't being stitched back together in an outpatient suite.

The ride back to my apartment is quiet. Carlos tries to talk to me a few times, but I am not in the mood. I shouldn't be rude, but I don't have it in me right now.

When we get to my apartment he comes around to help me out, guiding me out with one hand, my other resting on his shoulder for control.

"Thank you, Carlos." I start to try to walk, which is awful. Like dragging a weighted ball and chain behind me as I go.

"I can help you up the stairs," he offers.

"No, I got it," I holler without turning to face him.

Behind me I hear him grumble something I don't understand, then I hear his footsteps catch up, and he's standing in front of me.

"Sara, please let me help you."

He's looking at me with those big, honey eyes in a way that no one has ever looked at me. It both scares and fascinates me at the same time. He continues to go out of his way for me, I can at least let the guy feel appreciated.

A smile passes over his face, and the next thing I know he's scooped me up again.

"Oh my!" I try not to shout as I wrap my arms around his neck.

He carries me up the steps without breaking a sweat or changing his breathing. But my heart is pounding as I rest against his chest. The smell of him—summer, the woods, and sports—settles into my senses.

At the top he sets me down so I can open the door, and I sheepishly smile, "Thank you."

"You're welcome. Do you need anything before I leave?" His question takes me by surprise.

"No, but thank you. You have already done so much."

"Anything for a friend." He smiles before heading down the stairs, stopping at the bottom. "You have my number if you need it?"

I shake my head no and he nods, pulling out his phone. My phone vibrates almost instantly.

"Now you do, cariño."

Carlos smiles as he climbs into his truck and drives away. I watch him until he turns the corner and disappears.

If I didn't know better, I would say Carlos's beautiful tan skin looked a little pink in the face as he left. What did he just say?

CHAPTER 10

Miss Not-So-Independent

Carlos

Loving people well is a simple form of obedience, and I know how to make that happen. After I drop Sara off, I make three phone calls.

The first one is to Coach Emily to get the ball rolling. She has the women's resources in the bag, and she's had a chance to get to know

Sara.

"She won't ask for help, but she is going to need it," I tell her.

Coach Emily laughs softly, but not in jest. It's an honest laugh that recognizes truth. "That's because she still thinks asking is equal to weakness."

"I know, that's why I called you. She will need community, rallying, and God to get her through this."

"We'll fix that with a little Summer Breeze." Coach Emily has the type of smile you can hear through the phone call, Sara's going to need more of that in her life.

The second call is to my mom. She's run more meal trains than I can count. She's also my favorite person.

"Carlos! How are you, mijo?" Spanglish was the language in our Spanish household— my grandmother had insisted on it.

"Good, madre. But I am calling to ask for help. I am okay, but I need your guidance."

"Sí, mijo. What can I do?"

"I need to set up a meal train for a friend. What's the easiest way to do that?"

"That's easy, but first, is everything okay?"

"Yes, she just needs help."

"Oh, it's a woman?" The cheer in her voice when I say 'she' is humorous. Mom makes it sound like I have never talked to a woman before.

"Just a friend who needs help. She plays on one of the teams in the church league." Sara's blue eyes and smile pass through my mind, and I have to calm my own heart.

"Okay. I will send you an email link, then you fill in the blanks, and you'll be well on your way. Just follow the directions." Her cheery voice sounds like she won the lottery and didn't just tell me she was sending an email.

"Thank you, madre. I will call you later. Te amo."

"Te amo, Carlos."

Within minutes, her email arrives. I fill it out and copy the hyperlink it gives me for my final call—which is actually a text message to the Cornerstone Field League's group chat. I keep it simple.

Sara ruptured her Achilles. Surgery Friday. She'll need meals and check-ins the first two weeks. Let's be the community we say we are. Follow the link.

The response is immediate. Summer Breeze takes the lead, and the other teams quickly fall in line.

By midnight, volunteers have set up a calendar to be available to sit with her or run errands for her. By morning, the first week is full.

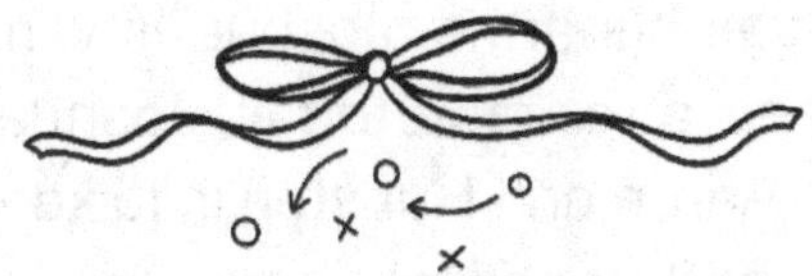

I think back to the way she pretended the boyfriend comment hadn't rattled her, but I saw it. I hadn't acknowledged the way her cheeks turned pink. The way that she had tried to swallow without being noticed. Or the way that she nervously twisted the ends of her long curly blonde hair in her fingers.

If I were honest with myself, after the initial shock passed, I thought for a moment about the boyfriend comment. She's still fiery, but in a way that calls to me. I have forced myself to refocus and pay attention to the details instead.

Full rupture. Surgical repair. Two weeks

non-weight-bearing. Boot with heel lifts to protect dorsiflexion. Gradual progression. Physical therapy starting around week two.

Remembering what Hannah said about how Sara's parents responded, I knew she was going to need all of us to get through this. I thought back to a battle in the book of Exodus where Joshua is fighting with the sword, and as Moses raises his arms, Joshua is winning. But when Moses' arms start to fail, Joshua starts to lose. Then Aaron and Hur step in to keep Moses' arms up, and together they win the battle. Moses supports Joshua; Hur and Aaron support Moses.

Sara would need us to be her support.

CHAPTER 11

The Cuts are Deep

Sara

Surgery day feels surreal. It started like any other day, but I knew I wouldn't be the same in a few hours. I tried to play it off like I was handling it well, but inside I was falling apart.

Emily drives me because I refuse to let Carlos take me anywhere else. Boundaries. I tell myself it's about boundaries, but it really is about how sweet and kind he has been—and how my heart does this fluttery thing when he is around, like I have never seen a man.

But when we make it into pre-op, guess who's already there? The talk, tan, honey-eyed ref.

He's sitting in the waiting area in his comfy gym shorts. They show off the muscular definition of his calves, and that golden tan he has. I quickly look away and take note of his cup of coffee and a book.

"You didn't have to come," I say.

"I know," he says with a smile.

Carlos always gives short answers, and I am not sure if it bothers me because I want to hear more from him, or if it's because I am protecting myself.

Emily squeezes my shoulder and whispers, "You've got a good one."

"He's not—" I start.

She grins and leaves us to grab coffee while we wait.

"You read?" I ask so the room doesn't feel so quiet.

"You don't?" The playful smile on his face gets me.

I see his point. That question was silly. "Okay, valid point. What are you reading?"

He lifts the book and shows me the cover. "The Bible?" I ask, partly caught off guard by his choice.

He nods with a smile on his face. "Need to get my time with God, and I understand we might be here a while."

"You're waiting all day?"

"Not only me, Coach Emily, and Hannah too. We are all pitching in."

I swallow the lump rising in my throat. I never had a support group back home; well, maybe I did before life happened. It had been a long time since I felt like I had people—not even a person—in my corner.

I open my mouth to say thank you when the nurse calls my name, and today gets under way.

When I wake up, my lower leg is wrapped

and elevated. It feels heavy, and that makes it real. I lie there a while, moving in and out of awareness as I come to.

Emily and Carlos are there when they wheel me out. She steps near the bed and holds my hand. "How you feeling?"

"Awful," I grumble.

"Repair went well," the nurse says. "No complications. Strong re-approximation of the tendon. Follow instructions carefully."

"We will." Carlos takes the papers, then hands them to Emily.

Once she reads them, she signs the discharge paperwork and they wheel me out. Carlos helps me into Emily's SUV before he leaves. I am not sure how I feel about him leaving. Sadness? Annoyance? Happiness? I don't know what I feel; it's probably the meds.

I am barely awake on the ride home, and it feels better when I close my eyes and lean my head back. I drift in and out of consciousness and thought.

This isn't what I expected when I left Texas. When I called Hannah to ask about opportunities in the area, she said her community was great, her church was the best, and I would love it here.

Yes, the community she had introduced me to has been kind and inviting. And the Church was—well, I didn't have a great answer for that yet. I had only been in a few times before the accident. However, it also hadn't sent me running away.

It wasn't that I didn't believe in God: I did. But I had been burned, and I wasn't settled in my faith. I had questions and needed answers, and I wasn't going to get them lying down.

But maybe that was the point; I never stopped moving. Perhaps this was God trying to slow me down to get some answers. Or maybe it was some kind of punishment for leaving Texas. Or maybe it was all a big accident.

I know this: I cannot think clearly right now.

CHAPTER 12

Already Taken Care Of

Carlos

Post-op Sara was different from the fiery, sassy football player she came off to be. Today she was subdued and reserved, but that was likely the meds wearing off. I know the timeline: twelve to twenty-four hours before the nerve blocker wears off and the real pain hits.

I let Emily drive her home. Sara and I had

spent a lot of time together recently, and that had pulled at some feelings I could only fight so much. But I also wasn't going to walk away. I also thought she would feel safer with a woman on her way home than me, not quite altogether in her right mind.

Hannah met me at Sara's apartment, with Sara's reluctant permission. The two of us work quickly to make last-minute adjustments before Emily delivers Sara home.

When Hannah opens the door, I quickly scan the space. There's a small couch and coffee table and a tiny dining table with two chairs that look more like they belong on a sidewalk in Paris instead of an apartment in Tennessee. Her place is meticulously kept, but sparse.

We clear pathways wide enough for crutches from room to room. We move the coffee table against the wall. We shift the couch so she can elevate her leg easily.

I set up a small side table within arm's reach: water bottle, phone charger, and remote. In the bathroom, I move her rugs, place towels for stability, and position a chair in the shower. When they pull into the parking lot, Hannah and I are finishing.

I help Emily get Sara up the stairs. It's slow but steady. I see the tension on her face in every movement. Everything feels new: stability, balance, angles on stairs, the way she looks at each of us like she doesn't want pity. But it's not pity, this is community.

I hold the door open while Hannah and Emily stand close to help if she needs it. When she makes it through the door, she stops and looks around; she notices immediately that everything is different.

"We didn't move anything permanently," I tell her. "Just enough to make crutch navigation easier."

She looks up at me. "You moved my rugs." It's not a question, solely an observation.

"Yes."

"And cleared the pathway to the bedroom?" She doesn't seem upset, but also not happy.

"Also, yes."

I see the recognition cross her face as she moves forward. "You've done this before."

My throat tightens, but I find my voice. "I didn't want you tripping over your own coffee table."

I see emotion rise unexpectedly, sharp,

and overwhelming when she sees the calendar with meals hung on the pinboard she keeps near her door.

"You planned meals?" She turns to Hannah and Coach Emily then, the surprise in her voice evident.

They offer her smiles and nod kindly.

"The team did," Coach Emily says, offering her a gentle touch on her shoulder.

She looks at the names written across the week.

Hannah. Coach Emily. Rachel. A couple of women I barely know. Summer Breeze and all the other teams.

"They like you," I tell her quietly. "Even if you argue with the refs."

A small laugh slips out of her mouth, and that makes me smile. But then I see her wince as the pain floods in.

"Why?" she asks finally, tears in her eyes.

"Because community isn't earned by being perfect. We build it by showing up," I tell her.

She swallows hard and looks away. That's when she sees the bathroom through the doorframe.

"You set up a shower chair?" she doesn't

look back at me, but I hear a shakiness in her voice.

Hannah speaks up then. "I thought it would be helpful, but Carlos set it up. I got to run, but I will be back later tonight."

"Thank you, Hannah," Sara says.

"I also need to get the kids from daycare, and then I will be back tomorrow morning." The two ladies hug Sara before heading toward the door, leaving the two of us alone.

Emily squeezes her hand before she leaves. "You're not alone," she whispers.

When the door closes, just the two of us remain. Sara leans against the back of the couch and rests the crutches at her side.

"I need to sit." Sara's pain creeps in around the edges.

"When was your last dose?" I ask her, even though I know, checking her awareness.

"Two hours ago," Sara says.

"Okay. We'll stay ahead of it."

The look on Sara's face when I say 'we' is surprise and perhaps some disbelief. I mean, the decision was already made for me, but if she tells me to leave, I will.

"How about you get comfy before your meds wear off?" I motion toward the couch.

She looks at me suspiciously but quickly gives in and nods.

"Bed or couch?"

"*Excuse me*?" She looks defensive.

"Would you prefer to be comfortable on the bed or on the couch?" I say it again with my hands raised apologetically.

"Right." She looks embarrassed at her assumption. "The couch looks comfy for now. Besides, I feel like I will be spending a lot of time in that bed soon."

"Couch it is." I smile.

I help Sara get comfy with a pillow under her leg, another behind her head, and her next dose of meds before I take a seat in the small chair nearby. She has her phone and slides through some screens before she sets her phone down close by.

"You prayed for me." It almost sounds like an accusation.

I don't deny it. "Yes."

"Why?"

"Recovery can be challenging, and finding peace in the journey will help your recovery."

She nods, but doesn't make eye contact with me.

CHAPTER 13

Day Two – Night Pain

Sara

The nerve block wears off at 2:17 a.m. I know because I'm staring at the ceiling when the pain hits.

It starts as pressure, then heat, then a deep, grinding ache that pulses in time with my heartbeat. I slowly pull in a breath and try to breathe through it the way I've breathed through conditioning drills and extra laps. But this is different.

It's not muscle soreness that will work out with a warm or cold compress. It's surgical trauma—repair and recovery. And I both chose it and didn't. Worst of all, there is truly little I can do about it.

I reach for the paper under my phone on the nightstand. My hands are shaking as I check the dosing schedule that Carlos typed out for me and left within arm's reach.

Ibuprofen, staggered. Prescription pain meds every six hours. Elevation at all times. Ice behind the knee, <u>not on the splint.</u>

He even underlined that part with another note: *Call if you need anything. -C*

I swallow the medication and wait.

And wait.

By the time it finally takes the edge off, I've been crying. I never cry out loud, but this makes me feel weak in more ways than just physically.

The tears slide into my hair because I can't even shift positions without help or screaming out. Hannah's sleeping on my couch, and she would come if I called her, but I don't want to wake her.

I moved here to be independent; now I can't even get to the bathroom without a strategy. The loneliness and the pain are fighting for control, and I want them both to lose.

CHAPTER 14

Minor Adjustments

Carlos

Hannah opens the door before I can knock. She looks tired, but smiles warmly. I hold up what's in my hands as a peace offering.

"I brought breakfast for the three of us." I hand over the drink carrier, and she takes it with a smile. "There's a tea for Sara—I had heard her say she wasn't a coffee drinker, and took note. I hope I picked the right kind."

"That's so sweet of you, Carlos," Hannah says as she sets it down on the table. "I am not sure if she is awake right now, but I will check."

Hannah knocks lightly before gently pushing the door open to Sara's room and disappearing into the dark. I set down the still-warm box from the local breakfast hole. They made the best breakfast burritos in town, but also had a healthy assortment of homemade pastries.

I had reviewed Sara's medication timing in my head on the way over. I've seen patients under-medicate out of pride, and I worry Sara would absolutely do that. But I also think she could swing the other way and over medicate to not be in pain. I am hoping, though, that she is somewhere in the middle right now.

Hannah reemerges with a soft smile and holds the door. "She's rough." Her arms cross her chest, worried. "But she's awake."

I nod quietly before grabbing the tea and the breakfast tray I had ordered for her on the way here. I take a deep breath before heading in, preparing for whatever stage she is in.

In the still-dark room, Sara is pale and exhausted, but alert in bed. I give her a quick assessment, walking from one side of the bed to the other.

"How's your pain?" I ask.

"Manageable," she lies through the grimace on her face.

"When was your last dose?"

She hesitates half a second, either because she doesn't want to say or she doesn't remember. I rattle it off before she overthinks it.

"You're due in thirty minutes. Take it in twenty-five."

She blinks at me curiously. "You memorized it?"

"I work with injuries, remember?" I remind her gently.

Hannah watches the exchange with interest from the doorway.

I help Sara sit up and adjust her pillows without asking before I check her toes for warmth and color. They are subtle circulation signs I don't comment on, but take mental note of.

"Non-weight-bearing means non-weight-bearing," I remind her with a smile. "No testing it."

She rolls her eyes. "Yes, Dad."

Hannah lets out a giggle from across the

room before Sara growls at her. Hannah hurries out of the room. But there's something in Hannah's expression when she looks at me: awareness.

Sara

Hannah had stayed with me all night, but I didn't call on her, not once. I didn't want to be a burden to anyone. Not even one of my oldest and dearest friends.

Carlos stayed for a while until Emily could get here. He said he left for a shift at work, but the way Hannah watched him moving around the room, I wondered what she was seeing through her eyes.

Before she left, though, she closed the door and sat down next to me gently.

"You know he likes you, right?" she whispers in the way you would expect a young school-age kid to, and not an adult.

I nearly choke on my water. "He absolutely does not, Hannah. He feels guilty that he was the ref on duty when this happened."

"Sara." She folds her arms and cocks her head. "He color-coded your medication schedule."

"He has medical knowledge," I pass it off.

"He reorganized your apartment," she points out the moved furniture.

"That's practical and makes sense for anyone post-op."

"He prayed in a hallway for you." That last one is a little quieter.

My throat tightens. "That's… new."

She smiles gently. "I know you haven't lived here long, but I have. Carlos is kind and generous, but he is also careful with people. He doesn't do this for everyone."

I look down at my splinted leg.

"I'm not exactly easy," I say out loud, and my eyes burn—not from the surgery this time.

"I think that's why," Hannah replies. "I think he sees something in you that you don't allow others to see."

I don't answer.

Because something inside me already knows she might be right.

CHAPTER 15

Day Four – Cabin Fever

Carlos

By day four, the swelling peaks and discomfort ramps up. Sara's frustrated, with cabin fever setting in.

She tries to "practice" balancing on one foot. I catch her mid-attempt before she can put her foot down or fall. Then she shifts her weight onto the injured leg—like she's testing it. The pain flashes across her face, and her knee buckles before she can catch herself. I am there to catch her before she hits the floor.

"You're going to re-rupture it," I say, sharper than I intend.

She glances up, then snaps at me, "I'm not fragile."

"I know you're not," I say, softer now. "But healing isn't weakness." I help her to sit back down and elevate her leg. She looks away.

"Sara, when you are cleared, I am happy to help you work through your physical therapy exercises to get you back to where you were. Back on the field, out for a run, whatever you want. But you have to do it the right way."

She looks at me with darts in her eyes, and I have to hold back a laugh.

"What's so funny, Carlos?" She is frustrated, and she gets this little crinkle in her forehead when she's mad.

"Nothing, cariño." It slips off my tongue before I can catch it.

"You were about to laugh." The look she gives me has an accusatory tone—the kind your mom would give you when she caught you in a lie.

"You really want to know?" I ask more to

see her response and judge if I should say what I am thinking.

"Yes, Carlos, I *really* want to know." She crosses her arms over her chest like she's trying to look tough.

"You're cute when you're mad." I wait for her to respond, but her body language rejects my words. I smile at her anyway.

"That's it?" Her sass level is high today.

"What did you expect?"

"Not that," she says, looking away again and twirling the ends of her hair that stick out at the end of her braid.

There's something shifting between us over the last few days. Less friction and more understanding.

When I leave that evening, Hannah walks me to the door.

"You're in deep," Hannah eyes me.

"I'm not." It's a lie, and I know it.

"You are." The smile spreads across her face.

I exhale. "She just got out of something."

"Believe me when I say, I know."

"She needs stability, not… whatever this is," I motion my hand from me toward her, glad we are out of her sights for this conversation.

Hannah tilts her head. "Maybe stability is exactly what this is, and you are exactly who she needs."

I don't respond to her, because I don't trust myself to be honest with my own emotions.

CHAPTER 16

Day Six – Summer Breeze

Sara

The whole Summer Breeze team shows up late one afternoon. Emily brings casseroles. Rachel brings flowers. Someone brings cookies shaped like footballs, and that makes me smile.

They all find places to sit in my small living room and fill it with stories and laughter. They talk about the first time they met me—the way I kindly but politely insult people on the field, but also how I am always the first one to help someone up and dust them off. The stories are sweet, kind, and definitely all me.

Within minutes, everyone is laughing, including me. On one hand, I wonder if they're being kind or if this is all because I'm injured. But I push away the doubt, knowing that it's not any of that. They really do care. For the first time since I moved here, I really feel like I belong.

Rachel and Emily share a short Bible study and a group prayer before they leave, since I will miss the next game—and the rest of the season after that. I hate this injury, but I am grateful they're here.

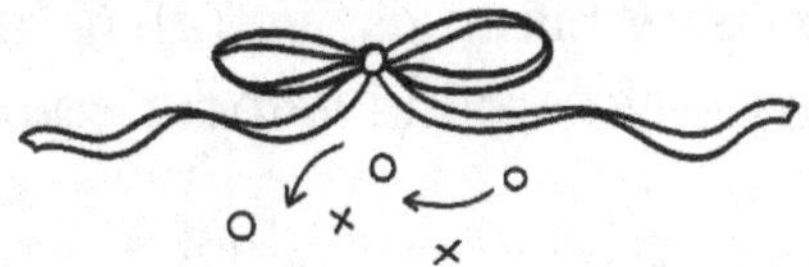

I'm exhausted, but lighter when the team leaves. Hannah stays behind to tidy up and sit with me a while tonight—since I am still not supposed to be up too much.

I watch her from the couch, where she's told me to stay put. But from here, I can see almost the entire apartment. Including the wonky cabinet door in the kitchen that is suddenly hanging straight on its hinges.

"What's that look for?" Hannah asks from the kitchen as she brings in drinks.

"Someone fixed the cabinet door," I say, pointing it out.

Hannah smiles. "Carlos did. He also fixed your porch swing after I told him not to sit on it unless he wanted to meet God." She swings the dishtowel over her shoulder with a smile.

I laugh out loud at that, but internally I am grateful for the trivial things. He wasn't asked, and he didn't tell; he just did it.

"I don't have the tools for that," I squint my eyebrows as I think about it.

"You saw his truck; you think a guy like that doesn't drive around without some kind of tool set?"

"Valid point."

Looking around the small room that was bare days ago, I see flowers, balloons, snacks, and a newly framed picture resting on the table.

"What is that?" I ask, pointing to it.

"Oh." She picks it up, examining the picture herself before handing it to me. "We thought having a picture for your place would be nice."

I almost burst right there; their kindness is beyond measure.

"I don't hate it here," I admit, wiping away a small tear.

"And Carlos?"

I hesitate and avoid eye contact. Hannah's known me too long to be dishonest. Even if I wasn't truthful, she would know.

"He makes me feel… steady," I say quietly. "Which is annoying."

Hannah grins. "That's called safety."

I stare at the ceiling, hoping my eyes dry out.

Safety.

I left Texas because I didn't feel safe—in more ways than one. Besides, being "strong" all the time got exhausting. I just didn't expect to not be strong here, especially not like this.

"Maybe you should take some time to pray on it," Hannah says as she plops down next to me.

"That feels heavy."

"Does it feel heavy because it's hard, or because you know that it's probably the best next step?"

"Can't that be both?" I grin and she

smiles back.

"Absolutely. I think there are days that prayer feels really heavy. But those are the days that I think I need to pray most. But I think there is a lot to be said about prayer. You never slow down, and now you have to. Take the time to reflect on you, your future, and God's plan for your life."

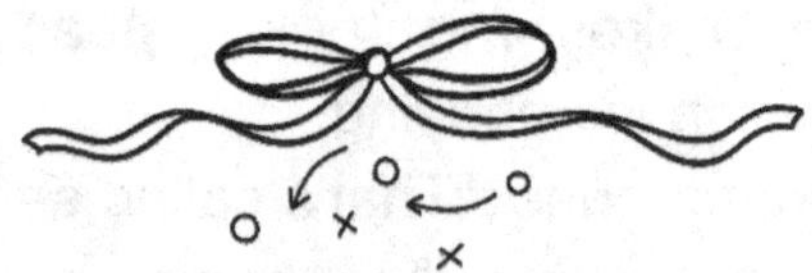

Before she leaves, Hannah grabs me a journal from the makeshift desk in my room. I write today's date in the top corner and start to write.

Dear God,
This feels silly, but I am here. I am not sure I can speak without crying. To be honest, I am not sure I can write without crying either.

This journey has been hard. I didn't want to move, but this place isn't bad. I am really grateful for this community. For the team, the league, and for Carlos.

I haven't done a fantastic job with picking men in my life. These flutters, the way he treats me, the way he loves you, all of that is good. I like that a lot. Do I act on this? What do I do?

Love, Sara

I look at the words I have written on the page and laugh out loud. It's not like God's going to pick this up and read it, but He knows the words in my heart. This was easier than feeling like I am talking to myself. Fighting back the emotions welling in my eyes, I close the journal and set it on the table nearby.

His note is still on my nightstand: medication, his number, a sweet note. I pick it up and read it again. His handwriting is gentle and easy to read, like the man I had seen in the last few weeks. On the field, he is a rule-loving ref. But off the field, he is gentle, kind, and caring. And when those golden honey eyes lock with mine, I get the flutters.

That's when I realize that somehow this stubborn, prayerful, compassionate man slipped right past my defenses without even trying.

CHAPTER 17

Day Eight – Texas

Carlos

I knock lightly on Sara's apartment door as I push it open at the same time. I freeze when I see a man standing in her living room.

He's well-dressed in a dark suit, wearing an expensive watch, and appears confident. Sara looks uncomfortable and out of place in her own space.

He turns toward me, assessing as he looks me up and down before speaking.

"And you are?" he asks in a deep Texas accent that lingers between disgust and resentment.

I almost tell him my name, but instead I answer, "A friend."

His eyebrow lifts. "Well, friend. I'm Daniel," he puffs his chest. "Her fiancé."

My chest tightens.

"Former," Sara says sharply, eyeing him like if she could stand on her own, she would chase him back to Texas.

He smiles like what she said doesn't matter. "We still need to finish talking," he speaks to her, but he's looking at me.

I step slightly closer to the couch instinctively, reading how uncomfortable she is. Daniel doesn't move, but the sneer on his face tells me he noticed.

"I still don't understand why you are here, Daniel," she asks.

"I heard about the surgery," he replies. "You didn't tell me."

"You forfeited updates," she snaps.

He looks toward me again. "So, this is who replaced me?"

I feel heat rise in my chest, but I keep my voice even. "That's not what this is."

Daniel chuckles softly. "Careful. Sara tends to outgrow people."

The words land heavily on her, like he knows where to press—and he likely does if he's the ex-fiancé. He looks back and forth between the two of us before he boasts something that shifts the room.

"You didn't tell him, did you?" he jingles his hand in his suit pocket like he's holding onto something powerful he's about to let loose.

He lets the silence permeate the space, watching Sara like he expects her to crawl back to him to keep his mouth shut.

"Tell me what?" I ask quietly.

Sara's face drains of color.

Daniel smirks. "You're still paying off the debt, aren't you?"

The room tilts.

Debt?

My mind races, wondering what that could mean, and what she might be running from. But *Daniel* can't help himself and fills in the blanks.

"You co-signed on the business," Daniel continues casually, then looks at me, trying to drive a point home. "She insisted she wouldn't let me fail."

I look at Sara. Her eyes are wide and she looks ashamed.

"I was going to tell you," she whispers, tears hanging in her eyes now.

My chest tightens in a way that feels unfamiliar. Concern. Financial entanglement. Emotional entanglement. Secrets.

How much of what I thought I understood about her was incomplete? Maybe Daniel is right, and she is still tangled in something bigger than I understand.

Then Daniel steps closer. "She doesn't need rescuing." He leans in and speaks to me quietly. "She needs saving from herself."

That's enough.

"Time for you to go," I say with enough bite to send a clear message that he is no longer welcome, but with enough grace to show who I am.

Daniel studies me for a long second, then shrugs and heads toward the door. He pauses a moment as he exits, looking back at me.

"You'll learn," the smile on his face might as well be from a snake. "She doesn't—" I shut the door behind him.

Silence still encapsulates the room, but it doesn't feel like the compressing space it was moments ago. When I look at Sara, she looks terrified.

"You're still financially tied to him?" I ask calmly, knowing it is none of my business. "If you don't answer, I will understand."

She nods once, tears about to pour from her eyes now.

"I didn't want to be a burden," she whispers. "Not even to him."

Something fractures inside me. I am not angry with her. But the realization hits that she's still carrying damage from someone who failed her.

"I need some air," I say quietly.

I step outside, but make sure the door closing doesn't sound like a goodbye. Sara sounds like she is in over her head, but I don't know her story—and it's not my place to judge. What I do know is that she's here for a reason, and my job right now is to help her through this obstacle.

I say a little prayer, ask God for wisdom, and get an answer: fresh air is good for the soul.

She's biting her thumb when I walk back in and I laugh. "Aren't you a little old for that?"

She tries to smile, "Some habits die hard."

I walk to where she is sitting and kneel down before her. "I don't know what happened in Texas, but I do know that God put you here for a reason. If that reason is for us to come around and support you through all of this, I am here for it. Everyone deserves a fresh start, so how about some fresh air to go with it?"

She stares at me for a moment before nodding her head lightly.

"Alright, give me your hand, cariño."

Her hands are cool to touch, but soft. When she gets to her feet, I hand her the crutches. She's gotten rather good at moving around on them. Today she looks like a pro as she makes it to the door.

On the deck, I help her sit on the swing before propping her leg up. I lean against the railing, looking out at the treetops ahead.

"This is harder than I thought it would be."

I turn to look at her, "Healing is always hard. Whether it is a matter of the flesh or a matter of the heart."

She nods, "I am not sure which hurts more."

"Well, prayer, fresh air, and a community

that cares about you, will stand by you through both." I kneel beside her again, "Can I pray for you, cariño?"

After a small nod, she reaches for my hands and I take hers. I bow my head and pray again, "Lord, my friend Sara is going through some things. She doesn't need to tell me because you already know. I pray that you are with her through this, and guide her in your ways. If those around her can help her Lord, I pray that you show us. Thank you, Lord. Amen."

When I look up, her eyes are still closed, but small tears fall down her cheeks. I reach up to wipe them away, and she startles before her hand comes to rest on top of mine, and she holds them there. She opens her eyes before mouthing a silent thank you.

We stay there: watching the Tennessee sun work across the sky while God works on her heart.

CHAPTER 18

Learning to Stand

Sara

Physical therapy is humbling. There's no crowd. No scoreboard. No adrenaline. It should be easy; just me, competing with myself. And Marsha.

Marsha says things like, "We're retraining the neuromuscular pathway." It makes me want to scream as well as think about all the ways I never want to be under these fluorescent lights again.

Today is partial weight-bearing day. Boot on. Crutches nearby. Heel wedges are still in place to protect dorsiflexion. I'm allowed twenty-five percent weight through the leg, and I'm not sure I know exactly what that is, but twenty-five percent feels like betrayal.

"Slow," Marsha says calmly, watching my leg. "Let your body learn to trust you."

My body doesn't trust me.

I lower my foot carefully. Pressure builds along the back of my ankle: tight, foreign, and fragile.

"You're safe," she assures me.

I shift more weight until my calf spasms. And I lose balance. Carlos catches me before I hit the mat. His hands are firm around my waist, steadying.

"I've got you, cariño." His words are quiet but supportive.

The words undo me, and I push away fast.

"I hate this," I snap.

Marsha puts her hands up to let me take a break before she steps back wisely. Carlos, on the other hand, doesn't react. He stays. Steady and dependable, unlike my Achilles.

"I can't even stand on my own," I say, my breath shaking, and then I start to unravel. "I was fast and strong. I built everything around that." My voice cracks. "And now I'm the girl who can't cross a room without asking for assistance."

The frustration spills over in tears. "I left Texas to start over. I had an opportunity here and landed a huge contract. Then this happened, and Daniel showed back up." I say that last part softly because, in my heart, I know why he's here.

Carlos has gone still, patiently waiting and listening. Carlos is like a sentinel, always watching, listening, and learning.

"Daniel didn't come because he cares," I continue, words tumbling from my mouth. "He found out about the contract I landed. I've got investors, and he wants access."

Carlos's jaw tightens, but he still listens.

"Daniel says if I don't help him again, he'll contest the loan paperwork as coercion. Drag it out in court and make it public." I sink onto the therapy bench, my whole body shaking.

"I never told you the worst part," I whisper.

Carlos moves close and kneels in front of me again.

"What's the worst part, cariño?" I still don't know what that means, but I am not going to ask. I like how it sounds when it rolls off his tongue.

When I look in his eyes, they are gentle and understanding—that relaxes me. "The business idea, the one that failed, it was mine."

Silence settles between us as he listens, and I am not sure what it means. Carlos is a good listener, though; I have learned time and again.

"He pitched the company as his," I continue. "But I built the strategy. The client model. The marketing. He wants back in now that I'm rebuilding it under my own name." I realize I've balled my fists and relax them, the blood flow returning.

Carlos's expression shifts from concern to something steady. He sets his hand on mine and squeezes gently. "He doesn't get to take from you twice."

The sound of his voice pulls me from looking toward the past and anchors me back in the present.

When Carlos offers me a kind smile, I feel

certain for a moment that I can do anything.

CHAPTER 19

Eyes on the Field

Carlos

Trauma and grief are something I am used to seeing, but watching someone lose their sense of identity in real time is different. Seeing Sara curl in on herself pulls on my heart in a way that nothing else ever has.

Daniel isn't just a manipulator; from everything she's told me since that first encounter at her apartment, he's an opportunist. But I see her getting stronger, and I know that he has underestimated her.

"You're not weak," I told her one night when she was working on being independent at her apartment. "You're in transition."

She had let out a humorless laugh. "That's 'churchy' of you. Like something a pastor would say."

Then she lets it all out, like the dam broke.

"I built my entire life on being strong! I didn't need anyone!"

This has been building under the surface; it needs to come out. If this is what she needs to work through it all, I'm here for it.

"My family loved the athlete. My friends adored the athlete. And my *fiancé* flaunted the athlete. Everyone loved the version of me that could win!" She breathes heavily, the emotions pouring from her body.

"Then the business fell apart, and my relationships fell apart with it. Just like that, it was gone. I was left with nothing but Daniel. Then he replaced me too."

I step by her side and place my hand on her shoulder. "I like the version of you that gets back up. Moving here was equivalent to you getting back up. You started over, and that's never easy."

She looks at me. "Even when I can't run?"

"Especially then, cariño."

She turns to the window and looks beyond the panes to the outside world. I know she craves to be back on the field with her friends. They had been pouring into her even off the field; they made sure she never felt alone. Calls, texts, meals that still showed up, and even a house cleaner they all chipped in to come help her.

"I'm serious, Sara." She doesn't look at me, so I walk to her side and set my hand on her shoulder.

"I've been thinking." She turns to look at me for a moment. "Would you be able to take me to the field Saturday? Since I am still not driving."

I smile at her. "I think your team would love that. It's almost championships for this season."

"If I'm going to be the injured girl, I'd rather be the injured girl who shows up."

"I would be happy to take you, cariño."

Something warm settles in my chest when she smiles, and a sparkle returns to those baby blues.

I didn't expect this pretty blonde from Texas to pull at my heartstrings so fast, yet here we are.

CHAPTER 20

More than a Player

Sara

Carlos brought a fold-out chair to the sideline for me in case I get tired. He carried the chair, my bag, and stood close enough to help me if I stumbled with my boot on the grass. When Summer Breeze sees me making my way across the grass, they light up like I scored a winning touchdown. They swarm me; careful, gentle, and loud with affection.

"You're coaching from the bench!" Emily declares as she tosses me a new team jersey with the words 'Assistant Coach' on the back.

I quickly pull it on over my head and pull my hair up into a messy bun to show it off. It feels good to have a jersey back on—even if I am not on the field with them.

Across the field, Carlos is talking with the other refs before the game. He glances toward me as he slides his whistle around his neck and smiles, and I can't help but smile back.

He's gone out of his way repeatedly since we first met. He's smart, kind, and the way he speaks to God quietly when he thinks no one is listening is sweet. Sometimes it's in Spanish, and sometimes it's in English, and sometimes it's in both, and it makes me laugh—like when he calls me that name: cariño.

His calm presence is warm and comforting—a nice counter to my high-strung type "A" personality. But today, when our eyes meet, there's something unspoken there.

He blows the whistle, and the game starts. Coach Emily has stepped in to play while I shout advice and plays from the sidelines—mostly on my crutches.

The women listen with intention and for the first time since surgery; I don't feel sidelined. I feel like part of something more; I feel included.

After the game, as the sun dips lower, everyone lingers for Bible study. Chairs are moved to form a horseshoe under the large trees. Sandwiches, orange slices, and water bottles are passed around.

"Today's study is from Hebrews 10:24-25. 'And let us consider how we may spur one another on toward love and good deeds, not giving up meeting together, as some are in the habit of doing, but encouraging one another—and all the more as you see the Day approaching'."

That hits close to home. This town, this church, this league have poured into me when I was just a stranger, and now they feel like family. I have never had to worry about being alone because I am not.

The crowd dwindles as everyone leaves after Bible study. Eventually, it's only Carlos and Ryan having some ref conversation while I watch from the truck tailgate, my leg propped up next to me. Ryan waves goodbye, and Carlos makes his way over and sits next to me.

The Tennessee sky is beautiful as the

sun moves toward the west. It's just him and me on neutral ground.

Carlos

She looks tired, but also full of joy. She coached from the sideline with that new jersey Coach Emily got her. The way her face lit up when they gave it to her, I could see even from across the field. She wore it with pride, a smile, and dignity returned to her.

Without the fiery shell she wears like armor, she looks smaller, but not weak. In the last few weeks, she's gained more than strength in her leg. I see it in her heart a little more every day too.

She smiles faintly. "I have had a lot of time to think, and pray." She looks at me. "I don't want Daniel to define what I build here."

"I have a feeling that you are getting stronger in more ways than that Achilles," I smile back.

She studies me. "You think so?"

"I do."

The breeze lifts her hair slightly, and I hold back the urge to push the little curl that's sprung loose behind her ear.

"You didn't run when you found out," she

says, like she is still afraid I might.

"I don't run from complicated," I reply. "Besides, we all have a past, cariño."

Her cheeks turn pink, and it's not from the sunshine she got today. When she looks down, a peaceful silence settles between us.

"I'm scared," she admits.

"What are you scared of?"

She shakes her head. "Feeling like I am always running from my past, and that it's keeping me from having a future."

"That's an honest admission. But I want to remind you that with God, your past is forgiven. And if anyone wants to come poking around about it, you have some friends to come by your side in prayer and lift you up."

"That means a lot, Carlos."

"Sara, the last few months getting to know you, watching you get stronger, the woman you have become is nothing to shake your head at. I would be proud to stand by your side if you will let me."

She looks over at me. "You mean what by that exactly?"

I turn toward her. "I mean I am more interested in you than a friend. And I would be honored if you would let me come beside you and get to know you even better and see what God may have in store for us."

"Carlos," the sound of my name is so sweet from her lips that it almost takes my breath away. "I would absolutely enjoy that. You've been so kind and supportive through all of this."

"May I hold your hand, cariño?"

"Only if you tell me what that means." She looks at me and I realize for the first time that her eyes aren't only blue—they're shades of sea foam, turquoise, and sapphires—and they're the most beautiful eyes I have ever seen.

"It's like darling or sweetheart," I tell her with a smile that pulls into my eyes. The pink that spreads through her cheeks around her own smile tells me all I need to know.

For the first time since I met Sara, there's a genuine gentle response on her face.

"Yes."

We sit hand in hand, peacefully watching the sunset beyond the Tennessee hills.

CHAPTER 21

The Message

Sara

It's not a knock at the door; it's a ding in my email—from Daniel.

Subject line: We Need to Talk — Urgent.

I debate opening it, but I am tired of being afraid of unopened messages. I say a little prayer before I click the message.

He's contesting the loan structure. Threatening that he will claim misrepresentation. Suggesting that since we were engaged at the time, some intellectual property could be considered shared.

Shared.

Daniel wants what he has always wanted: leverage and control. He wants access to what I'm building. My chest tightens, but not the way it used to.

My emotions teeter toward anger that has replaced shame, but I take a deep breath. Carlos is close by, and steps near me when he sees my demeanor shift. I show him my phone and he reads the message quietly.

He doesn't interrupt or explode—his reaction is completely different from how Daniel would have responded. Carlos finishes and exhales slowly.

"He's bluffing," Carlos says, a look in his eyes that says he's not going to let Daniel hurt me anymore.

"You don't know that."

"No, I don't, but," he smiles at me and sets his hand on mine, "I know intimidation when I see it."

His eyes are kind and thoughtful, and his smile warm and friendly. What gets me though, is the way he is attentive and supportive without making it feel like I owe him something.

"I don't want you fighting my battles, Carlos."

"I won't," he says calmly as he reaches over and touches my hand. "But I will stand next to you while you fight."

That lands differently.

The door opens shortly after Carlos leaves, and, to my surprise, Hannah comes in. Her sunshine demeanor fills the space, along with the tangy aroma of barbeque she's carrying.

"Hey girl!" She sets the food down on the table before she turns back to where I am sitting—right where I was when Carlos left. "Thought you could use something other than the casserole I know you've been eating all week."

"It smells like Texas," I tell her, taking a large whiff of the air.

"It's from a new place in town, and the owner is from Texas." She does this little happy dance on the way to set the bag on the table, then looks around. "No Carlos today?"

"He had something he needed to do. He's here often enough though," I attempt a smile.

"That look," she says, her own smile fading. "That's not the look I expected to see on your face this morning."

"Daniel sent me an email."

She rolls her eyes and comes to sit next to me on the couch. "Of course he did."

I open my email app and hand her my phone. She scans the email and shakes her head. She doesn't have to read the whole thing; she knows Daniel enough to know exactly what the unread parts say.

"Did you respond?"

"No. I was upset, but I didn't spiral."

She tilts her head, studying me. "That's new."

"It is. I used to feel like what he thought and said defined me. Like I had to cut back pieces of myself to fit in his mold or make myself better for him."

"And now?"

"Now I just feel…annoyed. Sometimes I still hear his voice in my head," I look at Hannah and she half-heartedly smiles. "It's unsettling. But I also don't feel compelled to answer him in any way, and I won't step back into his mold."

Hannah smiles at that. "That, my friend, is called progress."

A small laugh escapes my mouth. "Carlos read it too. And he didn't try to fix it or tell me what to do. He listened and said he would stand by me through this—and that he is not going anywhere."

Hannah smiles as she stands to help me up. "That's who Carlos is, and I would expect nothing less."

"It's nice—knowing that he will be there; allowing me to fight my battles, but willing to stand at my side when I do."

"Carlos doesn't need control to feel secure. He just… sees you, Sara."

"It's very different from what I am used to." I admit it out loud.

"Daniel needed you to feel small, so that he could feel big."

The honesty in that statement feels like a

gut punch, and I am not sure I am hungry anymore as Hannah pushes a plate toward me.

"He makes me feel grounded," I look up at her, and she nods.

"Don't run from that, Sara.:

I have been running for a long time. From Daniel. From Texas. From everything that didn't fit the version of me I had to be. But in the last few months, I have had to think about who I am, what I believe in, and whose I am.

"Carlos isn't Daniel. And I am not who I was when I moved here," I smile at Hannah, and it's pride that I feel in finding my own two feet— even if one of them is still a bit wonky.

"Have you prayed about it?" she asks, cocking her eyebrow at me.

"I have. When I first got hurt, I was so discouraged. But you, Emily, the ladies— Carlos—have all helped me to feel encouraged and really dive back into the Word." I look up at the ceiling and close my eyes to try to hold back the emotions that want to turn into teardrops and parachute down my cheeks.

"Even before I left Texas, I felt distant from God. As if the words Daniel spoke over me cut into every facet of my life, including my relationship with God. I was afraid I wasn't good enough because I wasn't perfect." Hannah reaches across the table and puts her hand on mine.

"Sara, you aren't perfect, but neither am I." Hannah's smile is reassuring.

"Something I heard at the church service we streamed last weekend really resonated with me. The pastor said, "We are all in process every day. And the process is not to be perfect, because it is something we can never achieve. But it is to be better than we were the day before. I felt that deeply."

"That is a good word."

Over lunch, we reminisce about home, our lives since high school, and where we hope our futures are headed. Hannah and her husband, Jason, are hoping to start a new business soon. But me? I just want to be clear of Daniel, keep seeing where this thing with Carlos goes, and get back on the field.

My mind and heart are steady, but now I need my body to cooperate.

CHAPTER 22

Seeking Counsel

Carlos

Five years ago, I would have moved forward with Sara alone. But now, I reach out for backup and counsel from a man I trust, Mark, the head of the church sports ministry.

He's coached for twenty years, mentored dozens of athletes, and seen more life off the field than on it. He told me when I first met him that the best thing I could ever do for myself as a man, husband, or father was to surround myself with other men in various stages of life so that anytime I needed guidance, I had a variety of people to choose from. Those people might offer varying opinions, but they would be speaking with wisdom. But today, he's the one I want to speak to.

We agreed to meet at a small café within walking distance of the church. There's a path that connects to the nearby greenway that winds from one end of town to the other. It's nice and quiet; a perfect place to meet.

When Mark walks in wearing shorts and an athletic polo, he looks like he came off the path from a run instead of from an office in the church.

"Carlos! How's it going, ref?" The two of us shake hands and pull into a brotherly hug.

"Good, sir. I am looking for some advice."

We sit by the window that overlooks the park across the street, coffee and water on the table.

"I need… dating advice," I tell him, and Mark gives me a knowing smile. "Before you go too far down whatever trail you have running in your mind, it's not about her. It's about her ex."

The smile vanishes from Mark's face. "I see. What do you want to know?"

"How can I help her with him, without being overbearing, but ensuring she is safe?"

"That is a loaded question, Carlos. In my experience, the most important thing you can do for her is to be there as a support—like you have been. Assure her that she is supported. More than that, though, pray with her, for her, and take her to church."

I let out a short laugh, "I had a feeling that's what you would say."

"One more thing: don't try to solve it for her. Let her take the lead unless she asks you to." He gives me that look that older men do that says, *been there, done that, and messed it up before.*

"I don't want to overstep, but I also don't want to stand by while he manipulates her."

Mark leans back in the chair. "Support doesn't mean control, and protection doesn't mean possession."

I nod in agreement before we pray together. For wisdom, for the future of the relationship Sara and I have entered, and for truth to hold up under scrutiny.

Afterward, Mark looks at me steadily.

"Encourage her to get legal advice. Concrete information, not emotional reaction. And remind her she's not fighting alone."

It's grounded and practical. Like my faith.

Sara sets a meeting with Daniel in a public place to talk through things. A local coffee shop that would serve as neutral ground. She asks me to stay close, so I do. I choose a seat at the counter across the room where she stays visible to me. Jason's agreed to come along as well. Daniel wouldn't pick him out of a crowd, and he would be a good voice of reason if things go sideways.

She's sitting at the table facing away from me, but I can tell she is fidgeting with the ends of her blonde hair. When the agreed time passes, she glances at me. I pick up my phone and text her:

Wait ten more minutes in good faith. Then we leave. Deep breath, cariño.

I can almost see the release in her shoulders before she covers her watch face.

The bell over the door rings when Daniel arrives ten minutes late, like he's trying to establish control by choosing the time on his own accord. He's wearing another suit but looks slightly haggard compared to the last time we saw him.

"You look like you are doing fine." He glances at her boot before sitting across from her.

"I'm healing," she replies.

He smiles thinly at her, like he's considering his next words. "About the business—"

"I've retained counsel," she interrupts.

His smile falters slightly, but a hint of arrogance slides onto his face. "You are overreacting."

"No." She calmly folds her hands in front of her, "I'm done underreacting."

A tense moment of silence passes between them. He studies her carefully now, sitting back in the chair, looking uncomfortable. Good.

"I won't co-sign anything else," she sits up tall with her shoulders straight. "I won't refinance your debt. And if you pursue legal action, I will countersue for misrepresentation and intellectual property theft."

His eyes narrow.

"I've documented every original draft, every timestamped file, every investor email. The concept was mine before we were engaged," when she says it, his eyes go wide. Inside, a sense of pride swells in me; she's doing an excellent job.

He leans toward her, like a wolf watching his prey. I sense Jason shift in his chair to check on me; I nod that I am okay, and he turns back to face the situation at hand.

"You've changed," Daniel tells her.

"You are right. I've started to heal."

Her words land and he stares at her trying to see if she is bluffing. For a long tense silence, they stare at each other.

I can't see her face, but I hope it is radiating the same strength I hear in her words. Because in his face, I see that he realizes she's not bluffing. Daniel realizes he doesn't have any leverage left.

"You always did overcomplicate things," he mutters, standing.

"And you always underestimated me,"

she replies.

Daniel pushes the chair under the table harder than he needs to, and I am on my feet before he can look in my direction. When he sees me, he looks back to Sara before he leaves without another word.

I move to Sara's side and sit next to her, reaching for her hand. They're shaking hard, but her face still looks solid.

"Are you okay?" I ask her softly.

She nods before turning to me, "I was so afraid he'd still have power over me."

"And now?"

She looks toward the door Daniel exited then back to me.

"He doesn't."

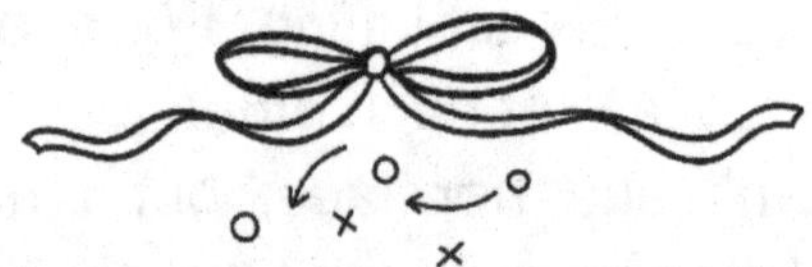

Jason tells Sara how proud he was of her for standing up for herself. Even though she hadn't been here in Tennessee long, we all could see how far she had come since arriving here.

After her nerves settle down, we walk into the afternoon light. She stops when the sun hits her face, looks up with her eyes closed, and a smile spreads from ear to ear. Her posture has changed, and it only adds to her beauty.

We follow her moment in the sun with a walk through the small shopping center. She hooks her arm through mine as we stroll. It's peaceful and quiet, other than the sound of her boot on the cement.

"You didn't jump in." She looks up at me.

I stop us in the shade of a tree and look over to her, "You didn't need me to, Sara."

"But you were there, and that means a lot. No one has ever been there for me like you were today."

"I told you I wanted to be by your side, and I meant that," I pull her in and hold her close.

"Thank you, Carlos."

"For what?"

"For not making me feel small or insignificant."

I pull back and meet her eyes. "You were never small, and you were never too much. You are enough."

She studies me like she's recalibrating everything she thought she knew about relationships.

CHAPTER 23

Truth Prevails

Sara

Carlos has been a gem. He's stood by my side through injury, surgery, dealing with Daniel, and is still showing up. Often I forget that I had a chapter with Daniel at all.

He's leading me across the grass to the pavilion where all the teams are celebrating the champions of this last season. Players, spouses, and kids of all ages. Many people here are athletes, but not all are believers. Today, though, Ryan gets to baptize two men who came to Christ through this league. That is a celebration in itself.

They've all welcomed me and are excited for Carlos and me to be dating—even if they keep teasing us a bit about the rules we have given ourselves to keep our relationship pure. But being around this group makes this place feel like home.

Carlos and the guys are setting out cones on the field for a post-celebration game when the email comes to my phone; it's my lawyer.

Ms. Keller,
I spoke with Mr. Gnick's
attorney today. After reviewing
the information you provided,
and your statements, his
attorney has advised they will
be withdrawing their claim
immediately.

Please let me know if you

need anything else.

Mrs. O. Polts, Esquire

I stand in the shade considering the impact of what she sent. Daniel offered no admission of his own guilt. There would be no apology. It's just a retreat.

"Cariño, are you okay?" Carlos approaches me casually, with no one else noticing among the hustle and bustle of the afternoon.

I hand him my phone, and he reads it, nodding once. "I told you he was bluffing," Carlos says with a hint of a sly smile.

I look up at him and grin. "Yes, you did."

There's a relief that washes through me. My body feels like it's able to let go of negative feelings it had been holding onto emotionally, financially, and even physically.

"I would like to pray." When I look up to Carlos, he smiles down at me. Today his eyes look less like honey and more like sunflowers; bright and yellow.

"I would love if you did." He takes my hand and steps closer. The space between us gets smaller—it's about privacy. Carlos always makes sure I have that.

"Lord, I am so thankful that you have provided for this door to close. Thank you for the sense of peace you have given me. Thank you to those around me who have shown me grace through this process. Thank you for Carlos; he is good. Amen."

I feel Carlos squeezing my hands gently before he whispers "amen."

"I am proud of you," he says before pulling me in closer and placing a gentle kiss on my forehead.

He hasn't kissed me before, but that was sweeter than any kiss I have ever had land on my lips. I feel my body relax in his arms.

His words are heavy in meaning, but light on my heart. We walk side by side with our arms around each other back toward our friends. The future feels bright. I am looking forward to what comes next.

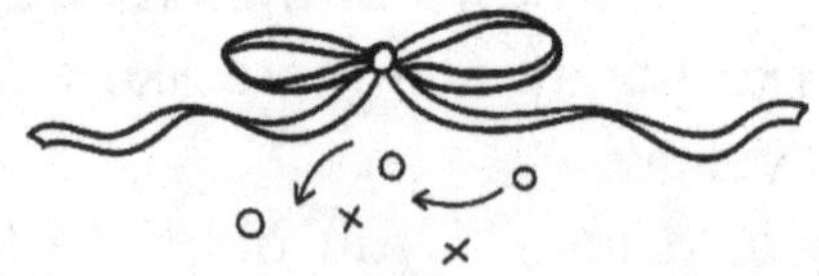

Carlos

Sara and I don't celebrate loudly or exclaim a dramatic victory for her. Instead, we hang out at the field after everyone else has left. Just the two of us and the fading sunlight. It's become our thing: tailgate down, ice cold sweet tea, and each other's company—and our Bibles, of course.

She's walking without crutches now. Boot still on, gait uneven, but improving. She can make it across the grass without me, but I like it when she hooks her arm through mine or asks for help. Her laughter when I scoop her up unexpectedly and carry her is the sound of joy, and makes my heart happy.

"Physical therapy says I'm ahead of schedule." She looks relieved.

"Because you listen now," I tease gently as I bump her shoulder.

She smiles at me. "I'm not afraid of not meeting anyone's expectations anymore." She owns that.

"Is that new?" I know it is, but I want her to keep talking.

"It is. I felt so trapped for so long that I also questioned whether I could do this on my own—start over and make something of myself." She looks at me, and the look on her face is full of gratitude. "You and all these people—my teammates, this church, strangers I have never met—have poured into me. It's been nice."

The field is quiet. No audience. No team.

"I just wanted to belong. I found friends, a church, and something else."

My pulse quickens when she looks at me with those beautiful blue eyes.

"I found you, Carlos. You were a stranger, then my friend, and now…c-carino."

I laugh at her, "Close cariño, but you need to put a little emphasis into it, change the shape of your mouth a bit." I lift my cheeks to demonstrate the over exaggerated shape, and after some practice, she says it successfully next time.

"The sound of that word coming from your lips is beautiful, like the rest of you," I tell her.

My finger rests gently under her chin as I tilt her head up. "May I kiss you, cariño?"

The smile that spreads on her face is gorgeous and makes this long-awaited moment much sweeter.

"Yes, Carlos."

Her lips are extra pink in the golden hour sunlight as I move closer to her and pull her face to mine. The kiss is gentle and calm, but also deep and intentional.

When she pulls back, she rests her forehead against my chest.

"You feel steady," she whispers.

"You feel strong," I reply.

And this time, neither of us is afraid of what's growing.

CHAPTER 24

New Playbook Rules

Sara

Green grass, spring flowers, and nerves I didn't expect to feel abound as I climb out of Carlos's truck. I've played this game since I was a kid. I know this game. But walking toward the sideline with cleats laced, green flags at my hips, and my Achilles wrapped in athletic tape beneath my sock, my body is shaking.

Nine months since my injury. Then surgery, crutches, boots, heel wedges, and physical therapy until my calves felt tight as dried leather. But that recovery didn't just work on my leg; it also worked on my heart.

I think back to a moment when I wondered what my path was, what God had intended for me. Now I know. He used that time to pour into me. Through my team, the church, this community, and Carlos.

Marsha cleared me last week. "Gradual return," she said. "Your strength symmetry is at ninety-five percent. Respect fatigue."

Respect fatigue, I remind myself, as I glance down at my leg. It feels strong, but I also remember its history. The shaking gradually stops as I work my way through the nervous energy.

"You ready?" Emily asks, squeezing my shoulder and bringing me back around.

"As I'll ever be," I smile as I catch the ball she tosses at me.

Across the field, Carlos stands in stripes, his whistle resting against his chest. But this time when he looks at me, he smiles. Not concern or caution, but pride.

Carlos

I've seen patients take their first steps after trauma plenty of times. But watching Sara jog onto the field—careful but confident—feels different. She's reclaiming the new woman she is. She's grown from the damage.

She stretches deliberately, no reckless bouncing. She's smarter now. Stronger in ways that aren't just physical and can't be seen—unless you know what her smile looked like before.

I see a moment of hesitation in her; the past creeping into her memory. Maybe her leg, maybe Texas, but either way, I am going to help her work through it.

"You don't have to prove anything today, cariño."

She looks at me and smiles. "I know, love. If there is something I have learned in the last few months, it's that I am not running away from anything anymore; I am running toward something."

Sara wraps her hand around my whistle and pulls herself up to kiss me on the cheek, and everyone hollers.

"No PDA ref!"

"Is that in the rulebook?"

"What play is that?"

Sara walks away with a smile and lines up with her team.

But when the whistle blows?

Game on.

Sara

By the third play, I forget to be careful. I am not playing recklessly—just free.

I take the handoff and feel the old instinct kick in. Cut left. Plant. Push. My leg holds, so I don't think about it. I run.

Not full sprint—not yet—but fast enough to remind myself who I am.

Speedy pulls my flag at midfield and I laugh.

"Good to have you back, Texas!" Speedy says with a smile before she jogs back to her team.

Carlos jogs past and makes a call, "Traveling!"

"That's not even the right sport," I shoot back.

"You're being dramatic," he says with a wink.

"You're biased." I put my hands on my

hips and the girls laugh.

This is us now. Not oil and water, but spark and steady.

Carlos

It's the fourth quarter, and the game is too close to call.

Sara makes a cut near the sideline and I call her out. She spins toward me and throws her hands up.

"I was in!"

"You absolutely were not," I taunt her with a smile.

She plants her hands on her hips, flags swaying. "I've been assistant coaching this team for months. I know the line."

"And I've been reffing this league longer than that."

She steps close to my chest, looking up at me and lowering her voice playfully. "You enjoy telling me what to do."

"You're on my field, ma'am," I say as I kiss her forehead, and she smirks.

"Remind me who wears the flags in this relationship?" Coach Emily hollers from the sideline.

I choke back a laugh as everyone in earshot laughs.

"Get off my field," I tell her playfully with a smile.

"Make me," she shoots back with a playful grin, her hair swinging around as she walks away.

I blow the whistle before I lose professional composure entirely.

Sara

It's the last play, and we are down by one. When Emily calls my number, I am ready.

We huddle, plan, and line up. Before the snap, I look at Carlos across the field. He doesn't soften, just watches.

The snap comes. I cut right, then pivot left.

There's a split second where fear tries to rise. What if it fails? What if it snaps again?

But my body remembers; I have trained for this. I step across the line. Touchdown, and the field erupts.

And for the first time since surgery, I don't think about recovery.

I think about joy and where the play God

called has led me.

CHAPTER 25

The Final Call

Carlos

I blow the whistle and the sound carries across the field like punctuation. It's game over, and Summer Breeze wins.

She's laughing when I walk toward her. Breathless, sweaty, and beautifully alive.

The girls surround her, hugging, jumping,

and celebrating. Sara is glad to be back on the field, and the team is glad to have her.

When everyone else scatters to pack up, Sara and I are left standing alone near midfield.

It's almost the same spot where she went down months ago. The moment where everything shifted and set her on a new trajectory.

"You made the right call earlier," she admits.

"I know." There's a little smugness there, but I deliver it with a smile.

She rolls her eyes at me but smiles big anyway.

"You did it," I say quietly.

She looks down at her leg, then back at me. She bends and flexes her leg like she doesn't believe it, before she turns to me.

"We did it."

I shake my head gently. "No, cariño. You did. I was there to cheer you on and be a pillar for you."

She studies me a moment. "You never tried to own my strength or recovery," she says, smiling softly. "Thank you for protecting the space around it."

I step closer to her and pull her close. Her

hair is up in a messy bun, her skin sun-kissed, and her turquoise Summer Breeze jersey brightens her eyes. Her freckles are bright as the stars starting to twinkle above. She studies me as I take in every detail of her.

"What is it Carlos?" she asks with the most precious smile I have seen on her face.

"I love you, cariño."

Her breath catches, and I see her read my face. First my eyes, then my lips, and the moment. "You love that I argue with you," she teases lightly.

"I love that you argue with me and still choose me," I tease back.

Her eyes soften then. "I love you too, Carlos." She rises onto her toes—carefully, balanced—and kisses me under the field lights.

It's not rushed or performative. It's steady, like everything we've built.

When we pull apart, she rests her forehead against mine.

"You're still biased," she murmurs.

"Probably, but you're mine."

Her arms around my neck gently pull me back down for another kiss, and I follow her in for it. "Definitely."

The field empties around us, and the

whistle rests silent against my chest. The two of us are standing here together, where it all started. And for the first time since I carried her into the emergency room, I realize something simple and sure.

Sara didn't need saving. She just needed someone that would stay and support her.

And with God's lead, I did. And I will.

THE END.

SNEAK PEEK AT BOOK 2:

Flags, Whistles, and the Unexpected Play

Emily

The kickoff game for the season had gone great. Summer Breeze was a full team again, with Sara back on the field, and a new recruit—CJ. The refs were their normal rule-following selves, led by Carlos. And I was determined this was the year we were going to win the championship for the women's league.

Last year we had been so close, but Southern Lightnin' squeaked one in and knocked us out of the last playoff game. Speedy—that woman was always quick, and that day she was on fire. Her coach, Mel, always knew where to place her to make a play. We were going to need a few new strategies if we were going to beat them this year.

Today I had come to the fields to "meet a

friend" at the pavilion nearby. Really, I was scouting the teams practicing today. There were seven weeks left to get ready for the playoffs, and I wasn't going to waste a moment.

I pulled out my coach's notebook and started scratching out my observations from previous games.

Southern Lightnin': Never forget about Speedy (Rylie) on a last play. Always look for Coach Mel to throw her signal (sign for fly) to Tara. Lizzy is a force (and Speedy is teaching her everything she knows).

Dragon Fire: Shiloh can throw deep down the field. Frankie will always go left; old injury won't let her go right. Coach Tanya pulls her ear when she's nervous about the field.

The Missionaries:…

"Coach Emily!"

Carlos's voice pulls me out of my notebook.

"Hey, Carlos!" I call back as he jogs toward me.

"Hey, I want to do something special for Sara. Do you have some time to meet with me this weekend to help me plan?"

"Of course. I can do Saturday after the games."

"That's perfect. My mom is coming into town, and I thought she could take Sara to lunch."

I raise an eyebrow. "Your mom? That's a big step."

"It is," he admits with a boyish smile. "But it's the right one. They've talked on the phone, but they haven't met in person yet. Florida's a little far for dinner."

"I wouldn't mind a beach a little closer too," I say with a grin.

He laughs. "Fair enough."

"Saturday works. See you then."

He waves and heads toward the parking lot, and I get back to my planning for the season. Who to play when and where. How to beat certain teams. Ideas for a new pattern.

"Excuse me, ma'am."

The voice is low and steady—like an old western drawl, but it still makes me jump anyway.

"I am sorry," he adds. "I didn't mean to startle you. I am looking for Pastor Ryan." The way he says Ryan sound more like R-ion and I have to stifle a giggle.

The sun directly behind him makes him appear as a silhouette and less of a person. But

I can make out a cowboy hat, the line of his shoulders—broad and relaxed, like he's not in a hurry to be anywhere but here.

"No worries," I gesture to the small shed near the field. "Pastor Ryan should be right inside that shed there."

"That so?" he glances toward the shed, then back to me before tipping his hat slightly. "Appreciate it. Have a good day, ma'am."

"You too."

There's something easy about the way he talks—and the way he called me ma'am. He turns and walks toward the building, unhurried.

"Huh," I say it out loud without meaning to. "Well, that's new."

I turn back to my notes and try to keep writing, but it all blurs for a second.

Cowboy hat.

Pastor Ryan.

I didn't see his face.

Not your average Tuesday evening around here.

I shake it off and go back to where I left off.

The Missionaries:…

But something about that interaction doesn't settle. It doesn't feel wrong, just out of place. Like a play that almost makes sense, but doesn't.

I glance back at him. He's gone. Like he was never there to begin with.

"Strange." I think I must be getting too hot, so I pack up my things to leave.

Walking to my car, I look over my shoulder one last time—the tug still there—but nothing.

"Alright, God," I mutter. "If that was something, I'm going to need more than a silhouette."

Something tells me that encounter wasn't random.

If you liked this preview of Book 2, you can preorder it on Amazon!
Thanks for reading!

ABOUT THE AUTHOR

Jenny Beth is a mom, wife, and lifelong military dependent who has called more places "home" than she can count. She grew up riding horses, hiking, and camping in the mountains of Alaska, Colorado, Montana, and Tennessee, where big skies and big-hearted people shaped her love of small towns and storytelling. A seasoned traveler who's moved around the country, she writes clean, faith-forward romance about resilient women, steadfast men, and communities that show up when it matters. Her stories are inspired by her own faith journey and by the ordinary heroes-family, friends, and strangers-who've left fingerprints on her life. When she isn't plotting porch-swing kisses and wildfire sunsets, you can find her chasing kids, planning the next trip, or hunting down the nearest bookstore.